A White Christmas in Berrycombe

A Heartwarming Romance

T N TRAYNOR

T. N. Traynor
Publishing

First Printed Edition, England January 2023

ISBN: 9798374962147

Cover created by Cristal Designs

This is a work of fiction.

Names, characters, businesses, places, events and incidents either are the products of the author's imagination or used in a fictitious manner.

Any resemblance to actual persons, living or dead, or actual events is purely coincidental.

My sincere thanks go to Nigel.

Without your eagle eye and polishing flare, this book would be found lacking.

Thanks for being such a great friend and editor.

Index

Index..4

Book Description....................................5

Bah Humbug!..6

Berrycombe...18

The Reason...31

The Berry Inn.......................................39

The Innkeeper's Daughter.....................47

Walker's Paradise.................................54

Storm Brewing......................................63

Old Man Down......................................75

Any Room at the Inn?............................91

Where's the Wise Men?.........................104

Tree of Love...115

Oh Ms Appleby!...................................126

Snow, Snow, Snow...............................136

Pylons Down..150

Make Haste for the Inn..........................158

Candlelight Nativity.............................173

The Holly & the Ivy.............................185

It's a Wonderful Life............................190

A Cup of Kindness...............................203

Author Information...............................215

Book Description

Only one thing can bring love into Carter's life – a Christmas miracle!

Carter decided years ago he didn't need anyone in his life. As a successful author with no need to venture into the world, he embedded himself in his comfortable Greenwich Village apartment and became a recluse.

After an unsuccessful year of writing, he decides to leave New York City for the holidays and go in search of inspiration. A remote country guesthouse in England seems like the ideal place for him to write his next story. He plans to hide away from yet another Christmastide and the painful memories it evokes. But some things are beyond his control. The fiercest storm in years is hurtling towards Cumbria. It will blanket the area with snow and bring everything to a halt, even bringing down the power lines and cutting off the electricity.

The landlord's daughter entices him out of his shell when she asks him to help keep the villagers warm. Carter is about to have his world turned upside down as the real reason for Christmas makes itself known.

Can Laura and the villagers melt his frozen heart?

A White Christmas in Berrycombe is a small-town, Christian romance with a whirlwind of festive magic and mistletoe!

Bah Humbug!

New York City

Christmas Eve, 2021

JACKSON SQUARE LOOKED MORE windswept than Christmassy. The coloured lights draped over the black, cast-iron railings did nothing to raise Carter's cheer. Standing in his warm apartment, the outside seemed somehow unreal; another world, a different time. Snowflakes drifted in gusts that blew through the city. They wouldn't stick, it was too warm.

Mesmerized, he watched one flake float in front of the window. As if being dangled on a thread, it jumped back and forth in an odd way. It fluttered forward and collided with the pane. He watched it slide down the glass to the ledge, turning to slush. The sight filled him with grief. The snowflake had lost its fight to stay afloat and now was gone, never to be seen again.

Is there any meaning to my life? Will anyone remember me if I cease to exist?

The thoughts made him gulp. They also made his mind up for him. For the first time in two months, he was venturing outside.

He hesitated outside his apartment block. *It isn't too late to turn around.* For a second, his hand reached for the door handle.

But then the image of a gift he'd spotted in a shop window on his last stroll came to mind. He pulled his woollen hat low to cover his ears and shoved his hands into the pockets of his black duffle coat. In a hurry, he set off down the busy street.

He huffed as he passed Manley's. Normally, he would go in and pick up a nice bottle of red. He hadn't been in since his last outing, and he wouldn't be going in today either. Not with all their decorations displayed with festive flair and gusto. He couldn't wait for the sixth of January when he could once more venture out without being assailed by holiday cheer.

'We've got six-footers,' cried the tree seller outside Jane Street Gardens to no one in particular. Carter hurried by. He kept his eyes fixed straight ahead and marched on with determination. He was finding it hard to remember why he'd suddenly had the urge to go out and buy Lizzie a present.

'Moment of madness,' he muttered to the ground as he rushed along 8th Avenue.

Do people even remember the true reason for Christmas anymore?

He hadn't been to church since he was ten, and even back then he'd never believed. After his mother… well afterward, he'd definitely had no faith in anything except hard work. Did all these people believe in the reason for the season as they rushed to fill up their homes with decorations, too much food, alcohol, and gifts galore? He was the opposite of a skinflint, but 'bah humbug' often fell from his lips during the Christian celebration of Christ's birth.

Arriving outside his destination, Cursive Gift Shop, he ground to a halt. The shop window displayed lots of multi-coloured miniature Christmas trees. An 'It's a Wonderful Life' banner hung across them, and all around the black framework coloured lights twinkled, winking at him and making him cringe. He almost turned around and went home. As usual, his present to his personal assistant had been a large bonus in her paycheck. He didn't have to go in. She wasn't expecting anything from him. Then he concentrated on the gift he had in mind. He gulped. It wasn't in the window anymore. *Do they still have it?* He could be in and out in three minutes so long as no one was being served before him and contactless payment was operational. He pushed the door.

It took much longer than he'd hoped. First, the present had to be found, having been put away to make space for Christmas gifts. Then the owner had taken delight in wrapping it in Christmas paper and tying a red ribbon around it. By the time Carter left the shop, sweat trickled down his back.

As he rushed home, he wondered when the dislike of people had crept into his life. Not that he disliked *them* per se, it was more that he hated being *around* them. He could like them perfectly well – from a distance. How had he let himself fall so far away from society? From the time he'd wound up in hospital on Christmas Day on his sixth birthday, he'd never liked Christmas. But it was more than Christmas these days, it was people. He didn't want to talk to them, smile at them, and definitely didn't want to shake their hands! Goodness no. The germs!

By the time he reached the park, a crowd had gathered to listen to a choir singing their carols with merry gusto. He nearly fainted. He became the Artful Dodger, and weaved his way around and through the crowd. *Silent Night* serenading him all the way.

When he was finally in the silence of the elevator, he took out a handkerchief and wiped his brow with a shaking hand. 'I sure hope you like this, Lizzie.' He looked at the bag within which sat the only present he'd bought in over twenty years. 'What was I thinking?'

After hanging up his coat and putting his shoes on the rack, he went into the living room and placed the present on the table. For a good long time he just stood there and stared at it. He couldn't remember the last time he'd wanted to buy anyone a gift. He considered it a puzzle. He'd ventured outside his comfort zone, but more surprising to him was the fact he'd wanted to. A shift had occurred in his DNA make-up. He could feel it. It was uncomfortable and alarming. His chest tightened painfully. He sat down quickly and laid his head back against the sofa.

His middle finger tapped his right thigh. 'I am in control. Everything is fine. I am in control. Everything is fine.' He repeated the tapping and mantra until his breathing returned to normal.

With it being Christmas Eve, Lizzie wasn't working today, but she had promised to bring some food he had ordered and would be here before three. Online shopping delivered the essentials, but he was partial to the cold meats and cheeses from Alleva's gourmet delicatessens and Lizzie had offered to collect them for him.

He made an espresso and went into the study. Originally, the room had been the second bedroom. He'd turned it into his workspace the day he moved in, eight years ago. Nothing had changed in all that time, he'd not even decorated. Lizzie often scolded him to either move out and upgrade or at least give it a facelift. Although he could afford it, he refrained from either. He told himself he didn't like change. But lately, he was wondering if maybe he was waiting; for what he didn't know, just something… different.

'OPEN IT THEN.'

Lizzie's mouth dropped open. Carter almost smiled. Maybe the trip out had been worth it.

'Is it a trick? When I pick it up, it's not going to explode on me or anything?'

Carter tried hard to muffle a chuckle. He forced his features to straighten up. Aiming to appear nonchalant, he stood behind the sofa and put his hand on it and crossed one ankle over the other.

Lizzie pierced him with a glare. 'If I open it and find a mouse in there, I'm handing my notice in!'

'Even a sugar one?'

'No… just a live one that could bite me!'

'I'm sure mice only bite as a last resort.'

'Seriously, is it a joke?'

Carter straightened up and let go of the sofa. 'If you don't want it I can take it back for a refund.'

'What, and venture out amongst the last-minute shoppers?'

'Well maybe not today, but next week when everything's gone quiet.'

Lizzie embodied the epitome of goodness. How, or better still, why, she had remained with him for so long was a mystery to him. This year she had become a grandmother for the third time and had asked to cut her hours to only two and a half days a week, wanting to spend lots of time looking after her grandchildren. Part of him believed she'd asked to go part-time because she knew both his sales and finances had dwindled lately. But she never mentioned that, and he'd gratefully accepted her new working hours.

In between throwing him piercing glares, Lizzie unwrapped the box.

'Oh!'

'Do you like it?'

In her hands was a snow globe. Inside the glass was an onyx sculpture of Mary Poppins, complete with a carpet bag in one hand and an open umbrella in the other. She turned it upside down and shook it. White flakes fluttered inside the glass ball. She turned the key on the side of the base and *Feed the Birds* began to play.

'It's beautiful.' Lizzie fought back tears.

A strange, warm sensation wrapped itself around Carter. 'Just a little something for my very own *Mary Poppins*.'

'Thank you, Grinch. I love it.'

'Pah! I thought maybe as I'd actually done something Christmassy you might drop the nickname.'

She shook her head. 'Sorry, no can do. You've been a Grinch for far too long.'

Joking aside, her words hurt. *What's become of me?*

Carter never portrayed his emotions, which made Lizzie do a double-take when she saw his face. 'Is everything alright?'

His blue eyes, framed by dark lashes and smooth skin, stared back at her unseeing for a moment. The thought flashed through Lizzie's mind (yet again) that it was a crying shame that someone so kind and handsome should lock themselves away from the world.

Carter shook his head and drew in a deep breath. 'Everything is fine. Now shouldn't you be on your way?'

Lizzie put the gift carefully back in the box, and then returned her worried gaze to his face.

'Now look what you've done! I'm all embarrassed because I haven't got you anything. It's your fault though, Grinch, because for the seven years I've been working for you, you've been pedantic about no presents.'

'It was a spur-of-the-moment thing, don't sweat it.' He couldn't tell her it had been a long, drawn-out agony of a decision. Nor that her smile meant the world to him.

Going against all his rules and requests, she rushed at him and gave him a brief hug. He froze. She backed away speedily before he took offence.

'See you in the New Year, Boss.'

'See you then, Mary Poppins.'

On Christmas morning, Carter had the grand total of two messages. The first one was a text from Lizzie.

Happy birthday, Boss. He deleted it.

Thirty-nine-year-old, lonely, dried-up author – not a tagline he particularly liked. He didn't need a reminder that time slipped by out of his control.

The other greeting was a card that had arrived by post last week. He'd kept it unopened on the table. He hesitated a moment and then picked it up.

Merry Christmas and happy birthday, Carter. We love and miss you. With prayers and blessings, Mom and Dad. He stared at it for ages. When he'd left home he'd been sure he knew what he wanted, and that hadn't included adoptive parents. Today, he was experiencing all sorts of thoughts and emotions. Normally, he would rip up the card and throw it away. This time he stood it upright on the table. For the first time in his life he admitted to himself that he was lonely.

New York City

December 12, 2022

'Here.' Lizzie tried to shove a gift-wrapped present into Carter's hands.

He wouldn't accept it and took a step backwards. 'You know the rule.'

'Well, you bought me one last year, so it's my turn.'

'But it's only the twelfth of December?'

'And? Christmas Day means nothing to you, and I want to give it to you before I go away.'

Carter accepted the small box and opened it. From the size of it, he guessed it was a pen. He would pretend it was just what he wanted, not that she would believe him because she knew exactly how many pens he had on his desk.

'It's not about the pen,' she said, as if reading his thoughts.

He took out an elegant black Parker. Silver engraving caught his eye.

Failure is part of success.

For a moment, time stood still. Breathing became hard. From last December to this, he'd not written a single thing. His life had frozen, and so had his words. He spent hours running on his treadmill instead of sitting at his desk. As a result, he'd become too thin, gaunt even.

'I didn't get you anything,' he croaked. If you could capture forlorn in a picture, then that would be Carter's expression right now.

'But you did!'

'I did?'

'Yes, the early bonus you gave me was enough to purchase this two-week holiday at Disney for me, my two daughters, sons-in-law, and grandchildren.'

'I'd hoped you would treat yourself with that money.'

'But I did! You have given me the most precious gift in life – time with my loved ones. You're a wonderful man, Carter Johnson, even if you are a terrible Grinch. Quite frankly, I'm glad you're going away this year, it will be more cheerful in New York for it!'

'Ouch!'

'Have you found anywhere yet?'

'Actually yes, I've booked a room in a guesthouse in England… for a month!'

'That's quite some time.' Her nose scrunched as she pierced him with her knowing eyes.

Carter shrugged. 'I'm hoping the change of scenery might help my writing.'

Lizzie gave a few short nods. 'I'm sure it will. You're a great storyteller, don't ever doubt it. But hey, if you're staying in a public place you're going to have to put up with Christmas!'

'As it happens, I won't. Look at this ad.' He opened a page on the computer and she peered over his shoulder.

The ad stated: Come and enjoy Cumbria, a walker's paradise, comfortable accommodation, home-cooked food, and beautiful scenery. Please note we don't do Christmas at The Berry Inn.

'That's got to be a joke?'

'No, I called Mr Hopkins, the manager, he confirmed he's serious, they don't celebrate Christmas.'

'Well, you'll be right at home then. More's the pity. When do you go?'

'Friday the sixteenth.'

Lizzie wanted to hold him. Although excited that he was finally leaving his apartment, she knew she would worry about him the whole time he was gone. 'It's a big step.'

That he had hardly stepped out of his apartment all year and now he was jetting off for a month? Yep, that was a big step. 'No big deal.'

Lizzie frowned.

'Trust me, I'm a big boy. I can do this.'

'Call me at any time if you need anything.'

'I'm not going to bother you when you're on holiday.'

She took a step closer to him, longing to wrap her arms around him. He pulled a face. She stepped back.

Lizzie started putting her coat on. 'Thank you for my bonus, it means the world to me to be able to treat my family.'

Carter got up to walk her to the door. 'Least I could do for the best PA I've ever had.'

'I'm the only PA you've ever had.'

'See what I mean? You're so good I can never let you go.' Carter's smile dropped. He might have to though if he couldn't get another book out there.

'Love you, Grinch.'

'Think you're marvellous, Mary Poppins.'

With her exit, the apartment plunged into silence once more. His hand hovered over the radio for a moment. Maybe a song or two might lift his spirits. He walked away without touching it.

Berrycombe

Cumbria, England

December 12, 2022

KEEPING THE HALL WARM these days was getting harder and harder. Further cutbacks meant they could only put the heating system on the lowest temperature, just enough to stop them from freezing to death!

'Keep your coat on,' she called to Penny who was about to undo her buttons. Penny smiled at her, and then went to sit with the others around the table. William dealt out Uno cards to everyone. Laura stood in the doorway for a moment checking the six of them had settled, and then headed into the kitchen. She propped open the door, so she could keep an eye on them. Legally she should have an assistant with her, but Emma had phoned in sick. Unable to leave the parents in the lurch, she'd opened the doors to the after-school club kids anyway. As it was just after seven a.m., technically this was the morning club, although no one called it that.

Anna Navarykasha and her children were here as normal, so at least that was another responsible adult. Anna glanced over into the kitchen just then, and Laura smiled back. Anna sat hunched at a table in the corner with her son and daughter, all of them colouring in paper Christmas trees to hang on the wall. The image caused a lump to form in Laura's throat.

Anna, Ivanna and Mykyta had arrived in Berrycombe just over six months ago. Her father had offered them a room at the pub and gone to great lengths fighting with the powers that be to get them over here from Ukraine.

When they'd arrived, they had been very grateful but subdued. Six weeks ago, just as they'd begun speaking English confidently and mixing with the other villagers, news arrived that Anna's husband Pavlo, had gone missing assumed dead. It had been a terrible day. Three days later, he had called them to say he'd been wounded but was OK. The children had hardly spoken since, and Anna was visibly struggling. Even though they knew he rested in a safer place, they still held their breath expecting bad news.

'Oh Lord,' prayed Laura for the umpteenth time, 'please bring some joy into their lives.'

Laura's father, Bill, had offered to help them find a permanent home, but Anna was adamant that they were going home as soon as the war was over. Bill accepted her wishes and gave them the two rooms at the furthest point of the large rambling building, to ensure they had some sort of privacy. Anna always tried to smile, but when the children were at school, Laura often heard Anna crying her heart out in their room.

'Time is a healer,' Martha Appleby would whisper. But her twin, Maeve, was always quick to respond with, 'Some pains are never healed, just bandaged over and noticed a little less.'

'Breakfast,' called Laura as cheerfully as she could. She carried a large tray into the hall and set it on the table. Steam floated out of bowls of porridge, and a colourful display of mixed fruit cut into bite sizes filled a large bowl.

The Navarykashas came over and joined the other children. They used to sit on their own to eat, but Laura had persuaded Anna that they would benefit more by mixing in.

The children piled honey, cream and fruit onto the porridge and got stuck in. Laura couldn't help a sigh. No one seemed to enjoy their food more than little six-year-old Matthew. He wolfed his down like there was no tomorrow, which made Laura worry about his home life. His mother, Joanne, was a young mum; a proud person, who Laura knew covered up the shadows of darkness in her life. Unfortunately, she'd fallen in love and married a drifter who left them on their own so much that Joanne might as well have been a single mum.

Nearly two hours later, the school bell rang. The children rushed off to their separate classes. Anna helped Laura tidy up and then the pair got in the car and set off. The drive home from Kendal only took twenty minutes and they soon arrived in Berrycombe.

The village had a grand total of fifty-three residents. There used to be a lot more, but over time the younger folk had moved away to more lively places. Now, if there were three cars on the road it felt busy.

'What are you going to do today?' Laura asked as they took off their coats and boots in the hallway of the back entrance of the pub.

'Bill agreed, yes. I to paint the hallw.w.w…'

'Hallway.'

'Yes.'

'It's a big task.'

'Tasssk?'

'Job, it's a big job.' Laura stretched out her arm to take in the vast, high-ceilinged hallway.'

Anna attempted a smile but it didn't meet her eyes. 'I like to do.'

Laura cast her eyes around. She couldn't remember the last time the inn had been decorated, long before mum died. It was dull and scuff-marked everywhere. A coat of paint would do wonders to cheer it up.

'You sure?' She nodded at Anna.

'Yes.'

'Let me know if you need any help. I'm a bit busy today but I'm free tomorrow.'

'Sure.' Anna went upstairs to get changed and Laura went in search of Bill.

'Dad?' she called entering the kitchen.

William Hopkins stood at the sink peeling vegetables. A bear of a man, with broad shoulders and a bit of a tummy, he was the cuddliest person Laura knew. She wrapped her arms around his waist.

'Hello love. Did it go OK this morning without Emma?'

Laura let him go and rolled up her sleeves to pitch in. 'Yes, it was fine. Anna was there to help keep an eye on them when I had to go out of the room.' She sighed.

'What was that for?'

'Matthew scoffed his breakfast down again.'

'Nothing wrong with a healthy appetite.'

'I know. I'm just worried that they might not have enough food at home.'

'Will you pop around and check on Joanne then?'

'Yes I'm planning to. I'm picking Joseph up in an hour for his check-up at the hospital. That normally takes two hours out of my day, and I have to be back at school by two forty-five. But I should have enough time to see her in between.'

'Is that useless husband of hers missing again?'

'Liam's not been seen in the village for nearly two months now, Dad.'

'That long? If he was my son I'd give him a right talking to.'

'You and me both! I know she struggles a lot to pay the bills, especially with all the energy price increases, but she's so proud she won't ask anyone for help.'

'Well, you tell her I said hello when you see her.'

'I will Dad.'

For a while they peeled and chopped up vegetables together in silence. This time of year carried sadness and both of them tended to withdraw into their own worlds a little.

'Do you think we should put up a Christmas tree this year... for Ivanna and Mykyta?'

Bill put down the chopping knife, and the two of them looked at each other. 'It had crossed my mind; they certainly could do with a little cheer in their lives. But I've spoken with Anna, and she says she is happy not to celebrate this year anyway. Plus, I have a booking from this American fellow and he was very clear that he doesn't celebrate Christmas.'

'So that's a no then?'

'I think so. We can buy some presents for the kids, of course. And I will be cooking a turkey for Christmas dinner, celebrating or not we all have to eat.'

'OK, I just wanted to check that's all.'

Her head bent down to carry on working.

'Laura?'

She looked back up again. Her eyes had filled with water.

'Do you want to put a tree up this year, love?'

She tried to smile and shook her head. 'Nah, it's too early.'

'It's been over four years now since your mother passed away.' He didn't add, and two years since Ethan left you, but the thought hung in the air between them.

'Still too early, Dad.'

He took the peeler out of her hand and put it down, then pulled her into his arms. 'We'll have to start moving on one day, love.'

'Just not today.' At thirty-three, Laura often felt that life had passed her by. She'd pinned all her hopes on Ethan, and since his desertion, she'd convinced herself she'd never meet anyone else and was doomed to become an old maid. Arthritis already nibbled at her joints on cold winter mornings.

THE DRIVE BACK FROM Penrith Hospital only took thirty minutes. It was long enough for Laura. She needed to fill in her time, and in helping others she found she spent less time thinking of her own woes. Still, Joseph Tanner tested her limits. If there was a 'grumpy old man' award, he'd surely win it.

She tried to have patience with him, reminding herself that his wife had died over twenty years ago and he hadn't got over the loss. Well, that's what he told everyone after three pints of Guinness! Laura had her doubts about the genuineness of his declarations.

His incessant moaning about *everything* paused only long enough for him to open the car door and get out. 'The council need shooting for not filling in those potholes yet! Me old bones are near worn away with all the jolting you gave me. You could have tried to hit a few less of them, 'taint like it's a busy road, weren't no other cars for you to avoid!'

'You'll be wanting to write the council a letter then, Joseph.' Laura pinched her lips to stop herself from grinning. Joseph's nickname (behind his back) was Mr Pen Pal, due to all the letters of complaint he sent out. Including at least one a month to the Prime Minister – whoever they might be at any particular moment in time, it was a bit hard to keep up!

'Oh don't you worry, I'll be getting my writing bureau open the minute I get inside.'

'You do that. Please don't slam…'

Bang!

'…the door.'

Laura rolled her eyes and sighed. Joseph was a test to anyone's patience. She watched him until he'd put the key in the door and opened it, and then she drove off. She had just enough time for a brew with Joanne.

THE DOOR OPENED A CRACK and Laura could see Joanne peeping out.

'It's only me, Joanne. I wondered if you had time for a cuppa?'

The door opened fully. 'Is Matthew alright?'

Joanne seemed to have grown thinner in the last few months. Laura had noticed some weight loss but hadn't realized just how much, until seeing her now without a coat on to hide her frame.

'He's fine. I just thought I'd pop around for a catch-up. I can't remember the last time we sat down together for a natter.'

Dubious, Joanne flicked her head to indicate Laura should follow her. Laura shut the door, took off her coat and boots and followed her friend into the kitchen.

The place, as usual, was spic and span. Laura was sure Joanne had just a touch of OCD. In all her visits she'd never once seen anything out of place, not even a single toy. The lack of money, of course, meant that Joanne couldn't overfill the house anyway. It had always been sparse, and the furniture that she did have had been picked up from the local hospice shop.

Joanne put the kettle on and put teabags into cups. 'Why are you really here, Laura?'

Laura wished she didn't have an ulterior motive for coming. Knowing she hadn't visited Joanne for a while caused guilt to niggle.

'I'm sorry it's been a while. I wanted to check if you're doing OK.'

Joanne kept her back to Laura, waiting for the kettle to boil. She poured water into the cups and stirred and still didn't answer. Laura fidgeted in her chair, beginning to wish she had come a lot sooner.

Tea made, and a cup in each hand, Joanne turned around. 'Let's sit in the front room.'

Joanne picked up the remote control and switched the television off. 'I guess you've heard that Liam's gone again.'

'No one has said anything, but it's hard not to notice when someone hasn't been around for a while.'

Joanne sipped her tea. 'This is the longest he's ever been gone.' Her voice cracked, and her chin dropped onto her chest.

Laura got off her seat and moved onto the sofa next to her friend. 'Have you heard from him?'

Joanne shook her head. 'It will be ten weeks tomorrow since he left. He hasn't even texted me once in all that time. I think he might have gone for good this time.' Her chin quivered and her shoulders slumped. Laura took her cup off her and put it on the table, then turned around and engulfed Joanne in a tight hug. Joanne released her pain in heart-rending sobs.

Laura was immediately wracked with even more guilt for not popping in sooner. 'Hush, hush,' she whispered over her friend's hair.

After a while Joanne pulled away. 'I need a tissue.' She made a dash into the kitchen and soon was blowing her nose like a trumpet. 'Sorry,' she said when she came back in.

'Don't be silly, there's nothing to be sorry about.' Laura put her hand over Joanne's. 'I'm here now. Tell me how I can help?'

ST MARY'S CHURCH stood towards the end of the tiny village. Over the years, the Church of England had threatened to close its doors many times due to lack of attendance and having no funds to make the necessary repairs. Each time the locals (even the ones who didn't come to Church on Sundays) had clubbed together, kicked up a fuss and raised funds to do the compulsory renovations. A great deal still needed doing, including a damp proof course, but it had been deemed 'safe' and so they could continue to use it.

A vicar came only once a month to conduct services. On the other Sundays, Emily (the churchwarden) would organize everything and do the best she could.

Normally, when the afterschool club had shut up for the night, Laura would head straight home to have dinner with her dad. Tonight she'd felt compelled to visit the 14th-century church. She dropped Anna and the children at home first, and then walked the short distance down the lane, crossed the main road, and entered the Yew-lined path up to the old building.

As a church helper and erstwhile Sunday school teacher, Laura had a key to the vestry door at the back. She let herself in.

The switch to the right of the door turned on the main overhead lights. She shivered. The building had always been cold in winter. Now it was freezing, the lack of funds meant the old oil fuelled heating system hadn't been put on in over a year. Little electric heaters – that did practically nothing, were switched on half an hour before the services. It meant the damp was having a field day and getting worse by the minute.

She pulled on her gloves as she walked into the nave, sure God wouldn't mind that her praying hands were covered up. She sat on the front pew and gazed up at the cross. She bowed her head and began her prayers.

She offered thanksgiving for everything she could think of: her dad, that the inn was still open after the terrible time of lockdown, the after-school club that earned her just enough money. She gave thanks for the National Health Service, for the council who tried their best to keep Berrycombe alive, and for all of her friends. Once her praises ended, she poured out all her requests for the village folk.

When her list of people dried up, she sat for a moment in silence. Since her fiancé, Ethan, had left her just before Christmas two years ago, she'd found it hard to carry on. She had thought they had been made for each other and his desertion left her feeling cold and empty.

She also missed her mum very much. Olivia had such a strong faith, and Laura missed praying with her and having conversations about everything. When Olivia died four and a half years ago, her dad had fallen apart for a little while. It had taken time for him to smile again, and even now she was sure his smiles never reached his eyes the way they used to.

'I think we need a miracle, Lord. What with Covid, the war in Ukraine, and now this financial depression, everyone is suffering one way or another. There is so much sadness around. It breaks my heart to see it all. Please send us a miracle... or two!' She took a tissue out of her pocket and blew her nose. Standing up she caught sight of a shadow on the wall. It made her jump.

'Oh sorry, sweet thing. It's only me.' Martha Appleby stepped into the light.

'I didn't hear you come in.'

'I was walking home when I saw the light on. I thought I would check everything was alright.'

Laura smiled. She knew Martha could see the church from her window and would have come over out of curiosity. 'Only me,' she said.

Then Martha did something quite out of character for the prickly spinster. She came over and took hold of Laura's hands in hers, raised them to her lips and kissed them. Patting Laura's hands she said, 'May the Lord grant every one of your prayers, and may He bring you, your very own miracle.'

The Reason

New York City

December 16, 2022

BUSINESS CLASS WAS A LUXURY. Carter had debated a good deal about spending this amount of money on his ticket. Last year he probably wouldn't have thought twice. This year not only had he been unable to produce another book, but the sales from his current books had dwindled quite alarmingly.

He settled into his seat, glad to be by the window. The last flight he'd taken had been ten years ago, when he'd flown from New York to Ohio and that had only been a one-hour, twenty-minute flight.

After his birth mother's funeral, he'd put travelling on hold. The sight of her coffin had stirred nothing but anger inside him. He'd been there only to take care of matters for decency's sake. Four people besides him attended the service. He'd spoken to none of them. He didn't want to know why they were there or what their connection to his mother had been. She'd been out of his life since he was six and this final chapter was the closure he needed. He'd only attended because the nursing home had him listed as next of kin.

When a passenger sat in the seat next to him, Carter kept his head turned towards the window and practiced the breathing techniques that Lizzie had persuaded him to learn. His heartbeat had been at top speed from the moment he'd left the apartment. The exercises helped a little. He laid his forehead against the cool of the window edge and closed his eyes. He would take the sedative the doctor gave him soon. In the meantime, he pulled his earphones out of his pocket, plugged them into his phone and listened to violins playing over the sound of crashing waves.

The plane's engines went up a notch as it began to push back from the gate out onto the runway. Carter's hands shook as he popped the pill and washed it down with water.

In his peripheral view, he noticed the passenger next to him looking his way. He purposely turned his head away. He didn't want to talk. He couldn't confess that it wasn't being in a plane that was freaking him out but sitting so close to a stranger.

Gratitude flooded him when the man reclined back in his seat.

An hour later the hostess asked if they would like a drink. In order to answer her he had to turn his head. He requested a red wine and as he went to turn back he locked eyes with the timeworn man next to him.

The gentleman instantly smiled, a hundred more crinkles filling his leathery skin. What could he do? He returned the smile, although it was forced and not very wide.

'Is this your first flight?' the man asked.

Of course the stranger would assume that was why he was shaking like a nervous wreck. 'First long haul,' he answered trying to deflect the real reason.

'It's amazing how quickly time will pass now we're in the air. We'll be in England before you know it.'

His accent was clearly not American. 'Are you from England?'

'Manchester, born and bred. And you... are you a New Yorker?'

'I am now, but I was born in Ohio.'

'Now there's a place I've always wanted to visit since I watched the documentary *How to Dance in Ohio*. Have you seen it? It's very inspiring.'

'No, I haven't seen it.'

'If you get a chance, check it out. It's about autism. The musical is worth a watch as well. Are you musical?'

'I play the piano.'

'How awesome! It's a gift to play any instrument I believe, but especially the piano. So what takes you to Manchester?'

'It was the closest airport to Cumbria.'

'Cumbria is God's playground if ever there was one. A place of renowned beauty so it is.'

The questions continued to spill forth from the stranger, and with them and the effect of the sedative that was kicking in, Carter slowly relaxed. To his astonishment, he even began to enjoy the conversation.

They stopped for a while to have a rest, and to eat their inflight meal. Carter settled into the quiet period with some relief. After the meal when the trays had been cleared away, he started flicking through the movie selection.

'You know another good film set in Ohio is *A Walk with Grace.*'

'I haven't heard of it.' He tried not to sound irritated at being interrupted.

'You should check it out if you're ever at a loose end.'

'I'll do that.'

'You know the *Shawshank Redemption* is also set in Ohio.'

Carter couldn't help but smile. 'How do you know all this stuff?'

'I've got a good memory, but I think it's more because the Lord put these in my mind that I have remembered them. Have you seen the *Shawshank Redemption?*'

Carter sank back further into his seat, putting an extra couple of inches between them. 'Yes, now that film I have seen.'

'Amazing story, don't you think?'

'Brilliant actually. I'm not a crier but I was moved.'

'What's your name, son?'

Carter's temperature chilled with dread. He might be talking, but he wasn't up to shaking hands. His palms instantly became sweaty. 'My name's Carter, but you'll have to excuse me because I don't shake hands.'

'Nothing to excuse. You know why we started shaking hands?' Before Carter could say he didn't, the man continued. 'It was to show the person you were greeting that you didn't have a weapon in your hand.' He lifted both his hands up in the air.

'No weapons,' he grinned. 'My name is Father Williams. But please call me by my first name which is Henry. It's nice to meet you, Carter.'

'It's nice to meet you too.' And the funny thing was – he meant it.

'For a man of the cloth, you seem to have lots of time to watch movies.'

'I do indeed. I've watched a great number of them on flights like this or in hotel rooms.'

'You do a lot of traveling then?'

'Aye, I do. The Lord has blessed me with the gift of the gab and I'm invited to talk at numerous events. People seem to like what I have to say because I'm often invited back.'

Carter shifted in his seat. He was not a religious man, never had been. He'd not stepped inside a church since his adoptive parents finally gave in and let him stay at home. He'd made sure his mother's funeral was held at a crematorium. The undertakers had organized everything for him, with strict instructions that nothing religious was to be said.

A part of him wanted to stop talking with this man of God, but a curious side of him was interested. Maybe he could incorporate this man's character into his next book?

'Is that where you've been? Giving a talk in New York?'

'Not this trip, unfortunately. A very dear friend of mine passed away, I was there for his funeral.'

'I'm sorry to hear that.'

'He's with the Lord now, and we'll have more great times when I join him.'

Whether the melting snowflake moment resurfaced, or whether the past year of soul searching had ignited his curiosity, Carter didn't know. But he opened his mouth and a question popped out. 'Why do you believe?'

Carter sensed the man relaxing as he smiled and turned in his seat to look at him.

'Faith is a gift from God, one which I often pray He will continue to give me in greater amounts. Tell me, why is it that you *don't* believe?'

'Huh!' There lay hidden inside Carter an anguish he clung to. It held residence within him and influenced his every decision. There was no way he was going to unpack it all for this stranger.

'It's not God's desire for us to hurt, you know.'

'But He allows suffering. Oh please, don't get me started. I think I'll watch a film now.' Carter started flicking through the movies, not really taking any of them in.

'What pain do you think is the worst kind of pain in the world?'

Carter looked at Father Williams, his eyes picking up the man's white collar that now peeked out over his jumper. 'Is any pain worse than another? I'm not sure. They say childbirth is very painful.'

'So it is, but women say the moment the child is born the pain vanishes almost immediately.'

'So... the worse pain is the one that lasts a long time?'

'I don't know, what do you think?'

Carter turned to look out of the window for a while. His thoughts flickered over cancer, wars, and famine. 'Hunger is a terrible pain.'

'It is indeed. When I see those poor blessed souls with their swollen bellies, it sends me to my knees in anguished prayer. But once food is given, surely the hunger pains vanish.'

Carter went back to thinking about all the different types of pains that the world experienced. An image of a Ukrainian mother sobbing over the body of her dead son came to mind. 'I think the loss of a child must be the worst type of pain there is. No one can take that pain away from you. I think it must stay with parents for the rest of their lives.'

'And yet, God so loved the world that He gave His only son so that we, that's you and I, should never die but have everlasting life.'

Carter turned his gaze to Henry and found himself locked within the man's light blue eyes that seemed to brim with life and truth.

'The Bible is nothing but stories.'

'So it is, stories passed down through time so that we might know the heart and character of God. I'm mighty grateful for the Good Book.'

'I envy your faith.' Carter wished he had something to fill him with such passion. He was envious of this man of the cloth, not of his faith in God, but for having a reason to live.

'If you can remember only one tiny piece of scripture, then I encourage you to learn John 3:16. It is the reason for the season after all.'

Carter breathed easier when Henry turned around and began to read a book. For a moment he closed his eyes and recalled last Christmas Eve. One of his questions had been answered. Of course, some people remember why Christmas is celebrated. But Father Williams was a sincere and devout man. *What about everyone else?*

The other question, which had filled his twilight hours with nightmares for the last twelve months, dangled in front of him like a neon sign – what gives *my* life meaning?

The Berry Inn

December 17, 2022

AFTER A SEVEN-HOUR FLIGHT, Carter chewed over the wisdom of picking up a hire car from Manchester Airport. Too late to change his mind now, it had been booked and paid for already.

The sturdiness of the black Wrangler Sahara reassured him. Plus it was under a two-hour drive to Berrycombe. He would arrive in the evening, but nevertheless he set off with confidence. All too soon he realized his error. They drive on the left in England. How had he forgotten that? It put his nerves on edge and he found himself driving the slowest he'd ever driven in his life. The cars behind him were sure to think that an old man drove the car!

Thank goodness for the navigation system that spoke to him in a loud, clear tone. He kept his eyes on the road and followed the female director precisely.

Above him a grey blanket filled the sky and cast the world around him in gloom. 'They look like snow clouds,' he said to the dashboard maps system. He turned up the heating.

'Damn!' Flakes fluttered through the air. 'That's all I need.' He flicked the windscreen wipers on. Cars zoomed past him. He knew he must be crawling along when even the heavy trucks overtook him. He'd thought the roads would have been a little quieter with it being a Saturday. He gripped the wheel and hunched over, concentrating on the cats eyes in the road.

He took the M6 all the way to Old Tebay and turned off. He had to backtrack south a little to pick up Pikestone Lane. If he'd been stressed before by the snow on the motorway, it was nothing compared to what he experienced now. The Wrangler filled the lane; he had no idea what he would do if he met a car coming the other way. Trees and bushes lined the way and obscured his view of what lay beyond.

'Why didn't I do more research?'

He broke out in a sweat.

Lights appeared in front of him and he slammed the brakes on. As he struggled to know what to do, the car in front started to reverse so he inched the jeep forward. The other car had pulled into a tiny layby. He waved as he drove past and the woman in the car smiled and waved back.

'OK, friendly natives at least.'

He thought he was ready to chuck up his lunch by the time he pulled into the tiny village of Berrycombe. 'What on earth possessed me? I could have been sitting in my comfortable apartment, or at least booked into a five-star hotel in Manchester.'

He drove right through the village and didn't find The Berry Inn. He found somewhere to turn around and headed back in. He passed a small shop and a few houses and then found himself out of the village again. He cursed as he pulled into the driveway of someone's house so he could turn around and go back in.

A tap on the passenger window made him jump. He pressed the button to lower the window. 'I'm sorry if this is your driveway. I'm a bit lost. You don't know where The Berry Inn is, do you?'

The old woman pushed back the scarf tied around her head and almost covering her entire face, and peered into the car. A pair of pale watery-blue eyes peeked at him, surrounded by a mass of deep-set wrinkles.

In a quavering voice she asked, 'Did you spot the church, young man?'

Carter nodded. 'Yep, I've passed it twice.'

The woman chuckled, making her thin lips wobble. 'You won't have seen it because of the snow, but opposite the church is a small lane. Turn in there and follow it to the end. You'll come out at the Berry.'

Carter sighed. 'Awesome! You're a life-saver.'

'Oh I shouldn't go that far, but you're very welcome.' She backed away from the car pulling her scarf back up over her short, grey hair.

'Nice woman,' Carter muttered to himself as he gingerly manoeuvred the car and headed back into the village.

Sure enough, opposite the church was a tiny lane. He'd seen it before but just assumed it only went to someone's house. A few minutes later, he pulled into a huge car park, which was empty except for two cars.

'Busy place!'

Made from dark brick, The Berry Inn carried a certain moody and derelict aura. Behind it a forest loomed, the branches of which were turning white. All around the property a waist-high dry-stone wall ran marking out the borders of their land. Overcome with anxiety, Carter couldn't get out of the car. He had wanted a deserted place to stay, so he wouldn't have to encounter too many people. But this looked very bleak and for a moment he could envision it in a spooky film. Yet he'd come too far to turn around now, and the snowfall had increased. He didn't fancy a drive back to Manchester in it at all.

He switched the engine off and got out. As he did so, two lights appeared in windows on the ground floor of the building. That seemed a bit more welcoming. *Maybe they'd noticed me driving in?*

He took his bags and suitcase out of the boot, and just as he was shutting it, the door to the Berry Inn opened. A man, standing with the light behind him, waved at him.

'Too late now,' Carter muttered and rushed to the building to get out of the cold.

'Welcome, welcome,' the man hailed him as he hurried through the doorway. Carter shrugged the snow off his shoulders while the man shut the door.

'Mr Johnson?'

'That's me, but Carter is fine.'

'Welcome to The Berry Inn. I'm Bill Hopkins, by the way.'

'How you doin'?'

'Grand.' Bill grinned. 'Did you find us alright? I know some navigation systems can't find us.'

'Mine couldn't, but a woman pointed the way for me.'

'Ah, that's good. And did you have a good flight over?'

'Not bad, a bit bumpy… but we made it!'

'Drop your bags there for a moment. I'll give you a brisk tour and then show you to your room.'

Carter hesitated; dog-tired, he'd have preferred to go straight to his room.

'Twill only take but a moment, we're not that big.' Bill grinned, and Carter put down his luggage.

'To your left here, we have a large lounge area for the pub. It's shut up because we haven't used it in three years. At the end of the corridor here is the entrance to the kitchens. If you're looking for me don't be shy to just come on in. Everybody does!'

'Let me show you where we serve breakfast.'

They walked down the hallway.

'Have you run the guesthouse for long?'

'I picked up the place thirty years ago. It's a freehold.'

Carter scrunched his forehead.

'Freehold means we're not tied to a particular brewery and I own the pub outright. And it's not really a guesthouse, more a pub with accommodation.'

'Oh, I see.'

Bill opened a door. 'We use this small parlour as the breakfast room. It's open from seven to ten each day.'

'Right, thanks.'

Bill closed the door and opened the door opposite. 'We converted this room a few years back. We call it the quiet room. There are desks in here, with lamps and all have electric sockets table-high so you can hook up your laptop. Do you have an adaptor, by the way?'

'Yes. I got a couple at the airport.'

'Good. It's amazing how many people forget to buy them. We have a few if you need any more.'

'I should be fine, thanks.'

'No one uses this room at the moment. My daughter and I have our own living quarters, and the only other people in the inn at the moment are a Ukrainian family and they hardly leave their rooms. So please feel free to come in here whenever you want a change from your room.'

'Sure thing.' Carter took in the clean room noting the well-worn state of the furniture. Loved but old sprang to mind. In fact the whole place looked a little bit lost in time. Only the hallway, which had been painted a magnolia colour, seemed to have a fresh appearance. It seemed a shame. Like something once grand was grinding to a halt.

He followed Bill down the corridor.

'This is the main bar. It's the only room open to customers nowadays. Only the residents see anything else.'

It smelt of burning logs mingled with slightly stale beer. Wooden tables and chairs filled the room, but not so it was cramped. More comfortable padded benches ran along the walls. Carter liked all the memorabilia that cluttered the walls, not one part left bare.

'An ode to Cumbria?' Carter asked nodding his head toward all the pictures that covered one wall.

Bill snorted a short laugh. 'I don't know how it started really. Someone took a photograph of the inn and my wife pinned it to the wall. Then slowly over time, more and more people started adding their snapshots. I've never had the heart to take them down since it was my wife who started it all.'

The tone of Bill's voice made Carter think that she was no longer here, but he didn't want to pry. Maybe that was the reason they didn't celebrate Christmas anymore.

He took in the rest of the room with a fleeting glance. A dart board hung in the far right corner and to the left of the room was an upright piano. Drawn to it, he crossed the room. A rosewood Richard Lipp original German piano. Two beautifully ornate candle sconces sat on each end of the piano front. He ran his fingers along one before lifting the lid.

'May I?' he asked, twisting his head to see Bill, who was standing in the doorway. Bill gave a nod.

Carter's fingers fluttered as he stroked the keys gently. With eagerness he pulled out the stool and sat down. Within moments his hands were flying and Beethoven filled the room. One key twanged and he cringed.

'Yeah, sorry about that. It's not been tuned in quite some time.'

Carter lowered the lid and pushed the stool back underneath. 'Who plays it?' he asked walking over to the bar.

'I used to.' Bill weighed up his new guest, his only paying guest in nearly three months. He decided to be open. 'I haven't played since my wife died four and a half years ago.'

'I'm sorry for your loss.'

'It was a long time ago, but thanks. Any road, let me show you to your room.'

Just as they turned to leave, Carter spotted a billboard on the wall above the bar, it said 'In God we Trust, everyone else pays cash.' It would seem the landlord had a sense of humour.

He turned into the hallway to follow Bill and bumped into someone.

'My bad!' he yelped, jumping back out of the way, hands in the air so as not to touch the prettiest woman he'd ever bumped into!

The Innkeeper's Daughter

December 17, 2022

THE WOMAN BLINKED SEVERAL TIMES. He liked the way her dark lashes fluttered, and her velvety brown eyes made him catch his breath.

'Excuse me,' said Carter.

'It's nowt,' she said taking a step back. 'All good here.'

They locked eyes and lost themselves for a moment.

Carter ran his hand through his hair at a loss as to what to say next.

'Any road,' the woman said brushing her jumper down. 'I'm just going to the kitchen. Best get to it before the stew burns.' Before anyone could answer, she charged off down the corridor.

'That…' said Bill scratching his head 'was my daughter, Laura. Come on. I'll show you to your room.' Bill picked up Carter's suitcase.

'I can take that.'

'Sure you're fine. You get the others, I'll take this.'

Carter followed Bill upstairs. 'Anna and her two children are at that end of the building. You're on this side. You shouldn't be able to hear them, but please let me know if the children disturb you at all.'

Carter knew he should affirm it would be fine, but honestly he wanted to write and the thought of children running around made the hair on his arms stand on end, so he stayed quiet.

'This is your room.' Bill opened a door and let Carter enter first. 'It's in need of a bit of modernization, but it's clean and should have everything you need. The mattress is new, so hopefully you'll find it comfortable. If anything doesn't suit you, please just let us know and we'll do our best to accommodate you.'

'Cool, thanks. I'm sure everything will be fine.'

'I'm afraid the drive to town might be a bit hairy in this weather. We can serve you some dinner here if you like, or the nearest town is Kendal. That's about twenty minutes away. You'll find lots of choice there. But if you want to stay put tonight, I can cook you a steak or you can try Laura's stew. She's made enough to feed an army, always does. Oh... you're not vegetarian are you?' His face dropped. 'Or vegan?'

Carter grinned. 'I eat most things, and I'm definitely not driving again today.'

Bill's face broke into a broad grin. 'Oh good! Well why don't you settle in, and then wander on down when you're ready for a wee bit of bait.'

'Bait?'

'Food.'

Where is this new world I've stepped into? I feel like I've gone back thirty years.

AN HOUR LATER, Carter made his way downstairs. His stomach growled loudly in response to the smell of cooking. He hesitated outside the kitchen door. Bill had said to just go in, but what if he should try the bar first?

Just as he was about to turn around and head to the bar, the door opened.

'Oh, hello.' A tall slim woman, with long straight hair stood in front of him. She had a large Roman nose and expressive eyes. 'You here in time to eat. I just going get you.' She smiled, but it didn't reach her eyes. This woman had sadness pouring from her every pore. Her clipped accent and chopped up English made it easy to guess that she was the Ukrainian woman staying here.

'I wasn't sure where to go,' Carter answered.

'Come to kitchen, it warm, no.' She opened the door wide inviting him in.

Bill, Laura and two children sat around a huge wooden table. The young ones looked curious, Bill grinned at him and Laura dropped her gaze to the table.

'Perfect timing!' called Bill. Come on in and join us.' Bill stood up scraping his large wooden chair over the stone tiles. 'That's unless you would rather eat in the parlour on your own? I can serve you food in there if you would prefer?'

Carter gulped. He didn't want to be rude, but… 'I'm very tired, so if that wouldn't be a bother for you I'd appreciate eating on my own.'

'No problem at all. Laura, why don't you go and make sure everything is OK in there. Turn the heating on etcetera.'

'Sure.' Laura stood up.

'I wouldn't want to put you to any trouble,' said Carter.

Laura finally looked up at him as she made her way over. Her face lit up with the softest of smiles. 'It's no problem.'

Carter followed her down the hall and into the small breakfast parlour. She flicked a large switch and the lights flickered and came on.

'Sit anywhere, but I would suggest near the fire.' She knelt down in front of a Calor Gas heater. She had to ignite it several times before the flame stuck, and even then she had to hold the ignition button down for several moments to ensure it stayed on.

'It doesn't take long to warm the room. It will be much quicker than lighting a log fire.'

Carter hadn't sat down yet. He fidgeted from one foot to the other and put his hands behind his back. 'I didn't mean to put you to any trouble.'

'Please relax; you haven't put us to any trouble at all. We're very glad to have you, truth be told.'

'Quiet times?'

'That would be an understatement. We've been dead in the water for three years now. We'll probably close at the end of next summer.'

'That bad?'

'Unfortunately, yes. We get lots of walkers during the summer who come in for drinks and lunch, and they tide us over for a while. But winters sap all our resources; we won't be able to afford to keep it open for another winter past this one.'

'I'm sorry to hear that.'

Laura sighed, then putting on a more cheerful tone she asked, 'What would you like to eat? We have sirloin steak, beef stew or I can make you up a ham and cheese salad if you would prefer?'

'Whatever that is, sure smells good!'

She grinned and her eyes sparkled. 'That's the stew. What would you like to drink with it?'

'You know I'm too tired to think right now. Why don't you bring me something that you think best accompanies the meal?'

After she'd gone, Carter sat down at a round wooden table near the portable fire and took in the worn carpet and faded wallpaper with its tiny floral print. Quaint and old-fashioned, it set his imagination running. Instantly, characters for a new story popped into his head. In his mind's eye, he saw a man and a woman enter the room. Their clothes gave the era away as the fifties. He liked the angle at which the woman wore her hat. Laughing and cheerful she didn't seem to suit the man whose arm she had hooked hers through. His large moustache resembled two bushy tails. For the first time in a year, Carter began a new story.

He offered a brief smile to Laura when she placed a glass of red wine on the table. She left him alone to start creating a new world.

His stew arrived with two hot rolls and butter. He couldn't help the 'umm' that came from him when he took his first spoonful. For the rest of it he was hardly aware of eating.

'Would you like some apple pie?' Laura asked when she came back in and picked up his bowl and plate.

He glanced upwards but it was hard to see her. In his mind, he was sitting at the table with a spy and a retired corporal. 'No thank you. I'm going up now. Could you add the bill to my room, or do you need me to pay now?'

'Dad said your first meal is on the house.'

'Oh, that's awesome, and appreciated.'

'You're welcome. See you in the morning.' She turned and left him alone with his characters.

'Yes I agree,' he said to the corporal with a slow nod, 'the waitress is undoubtedly an exceptionally attractive woman. The urge to run my fingers through her hair caught me by surprise!'

CARTER WORKED ON his laptop until nearly three in the morning. All tiredness had fallen away the moment he'd started writing. When he'd finally got to the stage where his eyes refused to stay open, he'd climbed into bed.

Even then sleep had been slow to come. His thoughts had switched from his new story to a pair of pretty chocolate brown eyes framed in a heart-shaped face and cascading rich-brown locks.

Walker's Paradise

December 18, 2022

AFTER A SHOWER and a shave, Carter made his way downstairs in search of breakfast.

The sound of Laura's laugh echoed down the hall. It quickened his pulse and temporarily fogged his brain. Bemused, he spun around and returned to his room. Weird sensations jumped along his skin making him shiver. 'Maybe I'm coming down with something?' He promptly kicked off his shoes and lay down on the bed.

Twenty minutes later and unable to either go back to sleep, or shake off the odd feeling, he got up and put on his Parka, hat and gloves intending to go for a walk. The fresh air, surely, would do him some good.

Five minutes later, as he rounded the bend in the corridor he bumped into Laura.

'Oh!' Laura wobbled.

Carter quickly put out his hand and caught her by the elbow. 'I'm so sorry. Are you OK?'

Laura's laugh sounded high-pitched and nervous. 'Yes, all good thanks. Nothing broken!' Again with the nervous laugh. She straightened herself up. 'You off out for a walk?'

'What gave it away?'

Laura giggled. 'I've got to be honest; you look like you're going on a polar expedition!'

Then Carter did something he'd not done in years. Her poking fun caused his deadpan expression to twitch until his guffaws filled the hall. 'Lizzie made me buy it!'

Laura's face dropped. She quickly smiled again, but it wasn't the same merry expression as a moment ago. 'Will you be long do you think? I haven't cleared the breakfast things away yet…'

'No. I'm planning a short walk around to get my bearings and then I'll be straight back. About an hour or so I should think.'

'That's grand. I'll leave everything where it is then. If I don't spot you when you come in, just pop your head into the kitchen before you sit down so we know you're in there.'

'Will do.'

Carter watched her as she walked away. He liked the way her hair was piled up in a messy bun at the back of her head. The wisps that fell down around her face framed her eyes perfectly. *She could be a movie star*, he thought as he headed out. *I wonder what she's doing here.* Then another thought came to him, *I touched her! And what's more I didn't mind!*

Carter shook his head trying to clear it. He hadn't wanted to touch anyone from the age of four-and-a-half when his dad had disappeared and left him alone with his mother. He shivered and set off down the tiny lane to the village. For all his long strides and rapid pace, he couldn't shift the image of Laura's face from his mind.

BILL CARRIED IN A plate containing a fry-up. Carter took a deep sniff of the bacon-rich air and looked forward to his first traditional full English breakfast.

'Would you like tea or coffee with that?' Bill asked.

'Coffee would be great, thanks.'

'Laura will bring it for you shortly; she's just back from church and has gone to change. She won't be long.'

Laura came into the parlour not long after Bill had left. Carter had devoured half his plate already.

'Great sausages,' he mumbled trying to quickly finish his mouthful.

'You can't beat Cumberland; they're the best sausages in the world.'

'I can't argue.'

Laura turned to leave. Carter shot out his arm and touched her elbow. A second touch, what was happening to him?

She turned back to him. He swallowed his mouthful. 'Do you know a good place to go walking? Somewhere not too far away.'

'They say it might snow again this afternoon.'

He grinned. 'I've my arctic gear to keep me warm.'

She tapped her tooth with a nail. Immediately he ran his tongue over his teeth. His cheeks coloured as he cleared away a piece of bacon.

'If you're determined to go today, I would drive down to Ambleside and then walk up to Rydal Hall. It's about three and a half miles and an easy walk. I wouldn't be going into the hills today if I were you.'

'That sounds like a plan.'

'It's one of my favourite walks. You hear the crash of the waterfalls before you reach them, and the views of Rydal Beck Valley and Nab Scar fells are magnificent. I never tire of it.'

'Why don't you come with me?' Carter immediately crumbled inwardly with insecurity and awkwardness. Why had he been so impulsive?

Laura leaned backwards a little, her face unreadable.

'Obviously if you're busy I understand.'

'You know what... I'd love to go for a walk today. Let me help dad clear up and prepare dinner and then I'll meet you by the front door. In about, say forty minutes?'

'Perfect.'

LAURA FLEW THROUGH THE tasks that needed to be done. She wanted enough time to change and check she was presentable before meeting up with Carter. Her dad sang along to *Dean Martin* as he worked. She threw him several glances, wondering where his high-spirits had suddenly sprung from.

'Sharon's not in today, Dad. You sure you're OK if I go out?'

'Of course I am. We'll only have the usual crew in this afternoon. Just be back before its dark.'

'Yes Dad!' She saluted him and then rushed out of the kitchen. 'Anyone would think I was still a kid!'

'You'll always be my bairn,' Bill shouted after her.

She rolled her eyes as she charged up the stairs. 'That man's got selective hearing!'

The Wrangler's suspension offered them comfort as Carter hit several potholes. 'Sorry,' he said for the third time.

Laura got the giggles. 'It's fine once you're on the main roads.'

'What are you doing?' Carter asked throwing her a sideways glance.

'Just paying for the parking. It's easier to do it online.'

He turned his gaze back to the road. 'Are you always this sensible?'

'Good Lord, no! But I'm learning. I'm a great believer in trial and error. I've received two fines for not having a parking ticket. I don't intend to receive a third!'

'So England is sharp on parking laws?'

'More now than ever. Since lockdown, we've had so many visitors to the Lakes that sometimes you can't find anywhere to park. You either have to give up and go home, or park miles away and walk.'

'Damn tourists, eh!'

'Can't live with them, can't get by without them!' They gave each other a smile.

As they drove, Laura cast him a sidelong glance. He was a handsome man, if you liked tall, dark males of the po-faced variety! Most of the time he was straight-faced which made him difficult to read. She rather liked his deep voice though, and found herself straining towards him whenever he talked. She wondered how handsome he would be if he would just smile a little more and relax. He always seemed on edge. She imagined him like an onion, with multiple layers that needed to be stripped back to find the real Carter. On one hand he was standoffish, on the other he'd asked her to come for a walk.

'Do people shorten your name? Should I call you Cart?'

'Call me Carter.' A muscle jumped in his neck. 'When anyone calls me Cart I feel like my mother's standing behind me.'

'And that wouldn't be a good thing?'

'No. I couldn't imagine anything worse.'

Laura wanted to ask him more, but his face remained stony.

The rest of the drive continued in silence. They parked, got out of the car and were immediately assaulted by a biting wind.

'You won't need that today. I don't imagine the mist will clear completely.'

Carter nodded, and put his camera back in the boot.

As they set off, Laura shoved her hands in her pockets even though she had gloves on. Earlier she'd been excited to accompany him, but something had changed and he'd withdrawn into himself.

They walked without talking. From under her fringe, she watched him taking everything in. She had tons of questions she wanted to ask him but he seemed aloof all of a sudden, more than before.

Eventually, she could stand it no longer. 'Is this your first visit to England?'

'Yes.'

That's it? That's all he's going to give me? 'Where did you go for your last holiday?'

'I don't normally take holidays.'

Laura almost tripped. He reached out a hand automatically but when he saw she was OK he whipped it back in again.

'Why don't you normally take holidays?'

'I'd rather not say.'

In an attempt to fill the void, she began to tell him everything she knew about Cumbria. She rambled on boasting about the county's highest mountains, Hadrian's Wall, the sixteen lakes and a stretch of wild coastline.

'The pace of life is calmer, the air is cleaner and the entire county is filled with beauty spots and a rich history.' She looked at Carter, but he still had his gaze fixed firmly ahead. 'You really should visit William Wordsworth and Beatrix Potter's houses. They're super interesting.'

Finally, he turned to face her. 'William Wordsworth's house is the main reason I chose Cumbria.'

'It is?'

'Yes.'

Shut down again. This was hard work! Laura begrudged the obligation she felt to fill the silence. His nods and occasional 'mm's' encouraged her not at all! Filling the vast emptiness with magpie-like chatter, (when she, herself, preferred entirely the sound of silence) grated on her nerves.

After another fifteen minutes of relating the historical life of Berrycombe she could take it no more. 'I'm sorry; my mouth seems to have run away with me today.'

'I could listen to you all day.'

She blinked several times. *Well blow me down with a feather!*

'You see, Miss Hopkins, I have lived in relative silence for years now. I thought I liked it, but your voice reminds me I have been missing out. Don't ever apologize for talking. You are who you are, and quite frankly I am glad of it.'

The rest of the walk to the house remained mostly silent. Occasionally, Laura would stop and be tour guide and point out particular spots. This silence however, was amiable. Carter's revelation had filled her with curiosity, but although she longed to know more, she was content that he had opened up a little.

She hoped that as the days went by he would relax even more, because she very much wanted to get to know him.

They arrived back at the inn at three o'clock, just before it started to snow.

'Good timing,' said Laura as they entered the hall.

They stood with the door open for a moment watching the snow sprinkle the trees, hedges and ground with a dusting of white. Their shoulders were inches apart. Laura had a sudden longing to take his hand, but kept hers firmly by her side.

'Can you excuse me, I must be going. It's ten a.m. in New York, and I promised Lizzie I'd give her a call.'

She shook her head as she watched him go the stairs. He wasn't that old but he spoke like a pensioner sometimes. *And who's Lizzie?* An irrational disappointment took away the warm feelings that had sprung inside her during the time spent with their American guest.

Storm Brewing

December 19, 2022

CARTER AWOKE WITH AN odd sense of excitement. He sprang out of bed, showered, dressed and went down the stairs with a light step. He stuck his head into the breakfast room. No one was there, so he headed to the kitchen.

'Good morning,' he called as he entered. His stomach dropped a little as he noticed Bill was the only one there.

'Good morning. You're bright and early. Would you like to sit in here this morning to have breakfast? There's only me and you around.'

'Yes, it's warm in here.'

'Aye, sorry about the cold. The bedrooms have central heating, but I'm afraid we never got around to putting radiators in the hallways. Take a load off.' Bill nodded towards the table.

After Carter sat down Bill asked, 'Would you like any cereal before hot food? And do you fancy a full English or something different this morning? I can make you an omelette if you'd like?'

'No thanks to the cereal, and a cheese and mushroom omelette would be good.'

'Not a big meat eater?'

'Not for every meal, it makes me sluggish, and I've got work to do.'

Bill cracked three eggs into a bowl. 'What sort of work do you do, if you don't mind me asking?'

Carter shifted in his seat. He didn't want to talk about himself. But he recalled the conversation he'd had with Lizzie the previous day. For an hour and a half she'd poured wisdom down the telephone line. She was the only person in the world he trusted, and he valued her opinion. But being open – well, that took courage. He took a breath.

'I'm an author. I've just started a new book actually.'

Bill stopped chopping the mushrooms and looked across the counter at him. 'I don't read much. I'm afraid I haven't come across any books by Carter Johnson. What type of books do you write?'

'My pen name is CJ Solace. I write murder mysteries.'

Bill dropped the knife down on the counter with a clang. 'CJ Solace! Well I'll be! I've got three of your books on the bookcase. I've not read them, I should add. Guests have left them here, and other guests pick them up to read during their stay. You're very popular!'

Carter gave a half-hearted smile before casting his eyes down.

'Ah, not good at blowing your own trumpet, I see.'

'Nope! To be honest, I'm not even good at conversation. Moving out of my comfort zone is testing me.' He blew out a long, slow breath.

Bill observed him as he poured the egg mix over the mushrooms. A rugby player in his youth, Bill had retained his muscle strength. A gentle giant, the villagers called him.

'When my Olivia died, I fell apart. If it hadn't been for Laura I don't know if I would still be standing. Her love pulled me through it. But for a time I lost myself at the bottom of a whiskey bottle.' Bill flipped the omelette. 'No one should live without people being part of their lives. We're not designed that way.' He put the omelette on a plate and passed it to Carter.

'We're all different, Bill.'

'Indeed we are.' Bill put some bread in the toaster and made them a fresh pot of coffee.

'Where is everyone?'

'School.'

'School?'

'Yep, didn't Laura tell you? She runs an after-school club in a school in Kendal. She does mornings and evenings. Anna helps her out a little in exchange for a free ride to school and breakfast. Anna likes to help out as much as possible, bless her heart.'

Bill's answer highlighted the fact that Carter hadn't asked Laura a single question about herself yesterday. He would have to remedy that.

'Her children are very well-behaved.'

'Ivanna and Mike, yes they're good kids. They don't disturb you, do they?'

'Not at all. I hardly hear them.'

'That's good.'

'Is their father fighting in the war?'

'Yes. He's in the army. He manages to call Anna and the children about once a week. He's fighting in Donetsk as Russian forces attempt to advance towards Bakhmut. Cell phones can be used for conversations only. Everything else is strictly prohibited. The calls are also being reduced as mobiles are being used to locate soldiers. Not good.'

'I wish that something would happen to bring the war to an end.'

'I think we need a miracle.'

'I don't believe in them. What we need is someone to take out Vladimir Putin!'

'And yet more violence never seems like the answer to me.'

Carter finished his breakfast lost in his thoughts.

Back in his room a short time later, he sat at the desk staring at the laptop screen.

Twelve years ago, his seventh novel became a bestseller on Amazon. After living in poverty for years, he'd been blown away by the amount of money that had seemingly appeared overnight in his account. A few months after his book *Incy-Wincy Murders* hit the charts he'd moved into his apartment. Over the following years he'd locked out the world more and more until eventually, Lizzie convinced him he'd become a recluse and needed therapy.

He hadn't planned this lifestyle. The only thing he knew for sure was that his characters meant the world to him and were more real than living people... except Lizzie. She'd kept him sane.

Last Christmas something had changed. The melting snowflake represented his life wasting away. He'd not written anything since, until arriving in Berrycombe that is.

A sense of adventure was building inside him.

He started typing. Several hours passed before he sat up and stretched in his seat, a contented smile on his face. This was going to be a great story. He never questioned why he called his main character Laura, or when dropping hints of her appearance into the story had described the innkeeper's daughter to the tiniest detail.

BILL WAS STANDING BY the window looking out, when Carter went into the bar in search of a coffee refill. Something in the man's stiff stance made him pause in his step.

'Is everything OK, Bill?'

The innkeeper turned around, his face ashen. 'They're not back yet.'

Carter strode over to him. The visibility out of the window was nearly zero. A dense snow storm meant they could see no further than three of four feet away from the building. He couldn't even see his car, which he knew was parked only a short distance away. 'What time were they due back?'

Bill gulped, and took out his mobile from his pocket. After checking the message, he looked at Carter. 'She sent a text at two-fifteen saying that school had closed early due to the snow and they were about to leave.'

Carter checked his watch. It was three-forty. 'How long does it normally take to get back?'

Bill turned back to the window and gripped the edge. 'Twenty minutes on a clear day, about thirty if it's raining hard... or snowing.'

'Do you think they went shopping before coming home?'

'No. Laura wouldn't have done that in a storm, plus she would have texted me if she had. She knows how I worry.'

'Have you tried calling her?'

'Her phone's going straight to voice mail.'

'What can we do?'

Bill turned around slowly. 'I'm going to go and borrow Alfred's tractor. It'll be slow but solid.'

'I'll come with you, just wait for me to get my coat.' Before Bill could argue, Carter went running out of the bar and up the stairs taking them two at a time.

He expected Bill to tell him to stay behind, but when Bill saw him, he simply opened the door. Wind whipped swirls of snow into their faces. They trudged across the car park, opened a small gate and went into a field.

The cold nipped Carter's nose turning it red. He stayed as close to Bill as he could, fearful of losing sight of him. Fifteen minutes of walking brought them to Tanner Farm.

Within moments of entering the farmyard, the heavy wooden farmhouse door opened and a black and white border collie came hurtling towards them, barking away.

'Cody! That'll do!' Immediately, the dog turned around and went to his owner.

'How'doo, Bill?'

'Be reet once I get me girl home.'

'Here's the keys. I got her out as soon as you called.'

'Thanks. Hopefully be back in a jiffy.'

'Aye.'

Bill and Carter climbed aboard the huge, green, two-seater John Deere tractor. Carter now understood just how sturdy the vehicle was. They left the farm and within a few minutes turned onto the road. Not that much could be seen of it, and Carter was glad he wasn't driving.

Anxiety gnawed at his stomach. He clenched his fists in his gloves. Surely they would be alright? Laura's twinkling eyes bore into his mind, so full of life. It was unthinkable that anything could have happened to her.

'How fast can it go?' he asked.

'Up to forty-five miles an hour, but we'd be crazy to attempt that in the snow. I'm keeping to a steady twenty.'

It made sense, but Carter found his foot pressing into the floor willing the tractor to go faster.

They hadn't passed a single car and he had no idea how long they had been on the road, when Bill called out, 'Up ahead!' He pointed and Carter bent forward, trying to peer through the blizzard.

It wasn't until Bill indicated and pulled across the road, that Carter finally saw the snow-covered red Fiesta. He took a deep breath. They hadn't crashed, that much was obvious as the car was fine.

As soon as Bill turned the engine off, they both jumped down and rushed to the car. The door opened. Mykyta and Ivanna got out first.

They giggled and shrieked in Ukrainian. Anna got out of the other side of the car. 'They say bless you for rescuing us.'

Carter was glad to see them all, but he was holding his breath for Laura. She got out last and locked the doors with a click. 'Knew you'd come get us, Dad.'

Bill gave Laura a brief hug. 'I tried calling you.'

'Sorry, Dad. My battery died on me!'

He shook his head at her. 'You know you should always have it fully charged. Come on, let's get home!'

'Hi,' Laura smiled at Carter.

'Hi.' His heart was beating a fast tune. An urge to hold her nearly broke down his years of isolation. 'What happened?' He said nodding towards the car.

'I'm ashamed to admit that I ran out of petrol.'

'It happens,' said Carter knocking his hands together to try and warm them.

'Come on!' yelled Bill, climbing the huge steps of the tractor.

The children squealed in delight and climbed the three steps up onto the tractor with the aid of Anna. Carter couldn't help smiling.

Being designed for two adults the cab was soon full. Anna and Laura shared a seat and put a child each on their laps. Bill got behind the wheel.

'You OK standing there, Carter?'

'Sure.' Carter squeezed in. 'We're not too heavy? Do you want me to walk?'

Bill laughed. 'City boys! No we're good, hold on.'

'We have new song!' said Ivanna. She turned her head to look up at Laura. 'We sing?'

'OK,' said Laura. She looked over at Carter, 'Cover your ears!'

Laura and Ivanna started together... 'On the first day of Christmas my true love gave to me...'

By the second line Bill, Anna and Mykyta had joined, 'A partridge in a pear tree.'

They had sung a few more lines when Laura winked at Carter, 'Join in,' she hissed before going back to singing.

To his surprise he didn't hesitate. Maybe it was the snow, or maybe the children, or maybe it was a pair of chocolate brown eyes... whatever the cause Carter found himself singing.

'...Four calling birds, three French hens, two turtle doves and a partridge in a pear tree!'

By the time they pulled into the car park they had just finished.

Mykyta and Ivanna asked Anna something excitedly in Ukrainian. She shook her head and spoke back to them. They tried to argue but she put a finger to her lips and they both went quiet.

Anna turned to the others as they got off the tractor. 'They want to play in snow. I say no.'

'It is *very* cold,' Laura said looking at the children. 'Besides I need your help in the kitchen. We have a gingerbread house to make!'

When the others raced inside the pub, Carter turned to Bill. 'Shall I come with you?'

'No, it's fine, get yourself inside. I'll probably stop and have a natter with Alfred.'

After changing into dry clothes, Carter went downstairs in search of a warm drink. Laughter floated out of the kitchen. Not so long ago the thought of being with people left him nauseous. Now, however, he headed into their presence with eagerness. Very strange!

Laura, Anna and the children stood around the large table, upon which sat a spread of gingerbread delights. Christmas carols came from the speakers at either end of the kitchen. Instead of cringing, he found the atmosphere surprisingly pleasant.

'Carter!' Laura jumped up. 'Would you like some hot chocolate?' She quickly went and switched the music off.

'I don't want to interrupt you,' he answered crossing the kitchen. 'And please don't turn off the music on my account.'

'Dad said you specifically checked that we don't do Christmas,' she said turning her head to look at him.

'Seriously, the kitchen is your domain for a start. Please turn it back on, I don't want to be a…'

'Grinch!' Laura smiled.

'Exactly.'

'I'm about to make a drink for all of us, so one more isn't a problem. Grab a seat.'

'You help?' Ivanna asked Carter with a sweet smile.

Her rounded, milk-white face was the picture of beautiful innocence. Her thick, dark lashes fluttered momentarily hiding her large blue eyes. With her long straw-blonde hair piled in a swirl on the back of her head, Carter thought she was an artist's dream.

'And how old are you?' he asked.

'Six.' She straightened up and raised her chin.

'Then I think you must be old enough to make the house on your own.'

'Suppose.'

Carter looked up and caught Laura smiling at him, before she looked down to pay attention to topping the hot chocolates with lots of marshmallows.

'OK, the icing is ready,' said Anna.

After placing cups in front of everyone, Laura helped hold the sides of the house together. Anna and the children began coating it with frosted icing.

'Thank you for this,' said Carter getting up.

Laura tilted her head and looked at him from under her fringe. 'Why don't you stay?'

'No it's alright. You guys have fun. I'll see you at dinner.'

Back in his room, Carter placed his cup down next to the laptop. Plots and characters had been flowing through his head all afternoon and he couldn't wait to write. Yet for a moment, he sat there and recalled the curve of Laura's lips and wondered what it would be like to kiss her.

Old Man Down

December 20, 2022

FRIGHT CAUSED CARTER TO wake up. His eyes shot open, and he stared at the ceiling waiting for his heartbeat to slow. Drawing in air through exaggerated breaths he willed his body to calm. Each exhale stilled his racing heart. It had been a long time since he'd last had a nightmare involving his mother.

'Man up,' he whispered, yet his eyes filled up regardless. He started tapping his thigh. 'I am in control. Everything is fine.' With agonising slowness his heart rate returned to normal.

He got up and dressed. No point staying in bed now, he was wide awake. Light poured in through the cracks between the curtains.

'Funny!' He did a double-take at his watch. Five a.m. Pulling back the curtain, brilliant white bounced up to greet him. It had stopped snowing, but everything was coated in a thick layer of fluffy white. 'Well you can't get more Christmassy than that!'

Wanting to get out of the bedroom and away from his memories, he collected his laptop, notepad and pens and headed downstairs to the quiet room.

He'd expected the place to be cold and dark but when he reached the ground floor he spotted a light behind the kitchen door.

'Great, I can grab a coffee now.' He went into the quiet room first and set himself up at a desk in front of the window.

He expected to find Bill, but to his pleasant surprise Laura was sitting at the table.

She glanced up. 'Good morning! Do you always rise with the larks?' She smiled at him as he approached.

His heartbeat increased, this time a pleasant light drumroll as he drank in her warm aura. Man! She grew more beautiful each time he saw her. 'I couldn't sleep, so I thought I'd come in search of coffee and start work.'

'Why don't I show you where we keep everything, and then if you ever come in and no one is around you can help yourself.'

'That would be cool, thanks.'

At the opposite end of the kitchen to the industrial cookers and stainless steel tops, a smaller kitchen unit displayed items more in keeping with a family kitchen.

'I believe in America you don't have kettles, is that right?'

'I don't have one, and I don't think I've seen them in the shops, but some people might have them.'

'Do you have to go out then, every time you want a coffee?'

Carter snorted. 'No. I have a coffee machine.'

'What about tea?'

'I have a small pan that I put on the stove.'

'We use the electric kettle here, it's easy. Just put in the amount you need,' Laura put some water in from the water tap over the sink, 'then you put it back on its pad and switch this button down. Easy!'

'Don't you have a coffee machine?'

'We have one in the bar but at the moment it's too expensive for us to run. I think we have a filter machine around somewhere. I'll ask Dad to fish it out. I'm afraid you've been drinking instant coffee since you arrived.'

Carter pulled a face and Laura laughed.

'It's not that bad!'

'I beg to differ.'

Laura chuckled. 'If you want to make a good cup of tea you should try using the teapot. Just pop three tea-bags in it and then fill up with hot water. Oh, but don't forget to warm the pot first and then to put the cosy over it when you've filled it.'

'Cosy?'

Laura picked up a knitted, brightly coloured hat shaped thing, with a pattern of black and white sheep on it. 'You pull it over the pot like this.'

'Ingenious!'

'Dad tells me you're a famous author.'

Carter stiffened slightly, 'Uh, huh.'

'Who has been your favourite character so far?'

Carter liked the question. Most people asked how he first got started or where did his inspiration come from. 'Scarlet, from the *A Fist Full of Revenge* series.'

Laura handed him a cup of coffee. 'Wow, no hesitation. What do you like most about her?'

His eyes narrowed ever so slightly. This was something he'd never told anyone, not even Lizzie. Yet, he wanted to share this with Laura. 'Please don't laugh, but I've been a little in love with Scarlet from her creation.'

'Really?' Laura searched his face. 'Are you joking?'

'Yeah, I know. It sounds crazy.'

'Not really,' said Laura sitting down at the table.

Carter joined her. 'You don't think I should be locked up then?'

'No. I get it. How can you expect your readers to love or hate your characters if you don't? Tell me what it is you specifically love about her.'

Carter put his elbows on the table and leaned forward. 'She's feisty and fiercely protective of the people she loves. She doesn't take any nonsense from anyone and speaks her mind without filters. She's also capable of love and lifelong commitment. Of course she also put poison into Ron's cake and stabbed Joseph in the back, oh and she twists the police inspector around her little finger!'

'Now that is some character! Did you base her on anyone?'

'No, she just kind of grew the more I wrote.'

'Do you base your villains on anyone? I read *Murder Most Sweet*, I think Mrs Craven will stay with me for years, very frightening antagonist!'

Carter sat back in his chair and took his hands off the table and placed them on his lap.

Laura's eyes widened a little in surprise. 'Writer's secrets?' she said trying to soften the suddenly tense atmosphere.

A force beyond his control flooded his chest pushing upwards, forcing words out of him. 'My mother.'

'Oh!' For a moment Laura let what he'd said sink in. 'Oh!' she repeated when she fully grasped what Mrs Craven had done. Words escaped Laura like a whisper of frightened awe, 'She tried to kill her son.'

Carter stood with a start, knocking the chair over. 'Sorry,' he said bending to pick it up.

Laura stood. 'Please don't go.'

'I got up early to write, please excuse me.' He bolted from the kitchen taking his coffee with him.

Laura sat down overcome with sadness. 'Poor man,' she said as tears filled her eyes.

CARTER COULDN'T WRITE. He found himself pacing the room instead. Why had he told Laura that? It was beyond him. He wanted nothing more than to run away, get on a plane and go home to his safe apartment. Why had he told her? He thumped the wall.

Several times he went to the door and put his hand on the handle, but he couldn't open it. Couldn't return to the kitchen and ask her to forget what he'd said. He sat down at the desk and glared at the laptop screen. The only person he'd ever talked to about his mother was the therapist Lizzie had found for him. Even then it had taken several sessions before she'd prized his memories out of him. What was it about *this* pretty brunette that made him want to reveal his soul? And why did he have the urge to touch her?

He started writing. Anxiety poured through his fingers as he created his new characters.

A gentle tap on the door made him glance at the clock on the laptop. Eight-forty, where had time gone?

The door opened allowing a rush of cool air to swoosh in and dilute the warmth from the fire. Laura gave him a tentative smile. 'We're just about to cook sausages to make toasties for everyone. I wondered if you would like one. Or would you prefer to go to the breakfast room when you're ready?'

He stood up. His heart played a retreat tattoo with heavy beats. He froze and his temperature dropped, causing him to shiver. He wanted to talk to her but his throat constricted making words impossible.

She rushed across the room and placed a hand on his arm. 'Carter, are you alright?'

Short, jerky nods his only response. His wide eyes implored her. Not knowing his aversion to touch, she wrapped an arm around his waist and guided him back into his seat.

'Are you ill? Do you have medication to take? Do you need me to fetch it?' She crouched before him and tried to take his hand in hers. He pulled it back, his body now shaking.

'I'm going to fetch dad.'

As she straightened up, he grabbed her arm making her jump.

'Don't.'

'Are you ill?'

He shook his head.

'Do you need any medication or anything? What about a drink of water?'

He let go of her arm and dropped his head forward.

'I really should get my dad.'

'I'll be alright in a minute, please stay.'

'I'm worried about you.'

'If you don't mind, you could fetch my tablets? They're on the bedside cabinet.'

'I'll be right back.'

She flew up the stairs but when she went to open the door it was locked. She raced back down again.

Carter offered her a weak smile and held up the key.

'Won't be a minute.' And off she went again.

He started tapping his right thigh. 'I am in control. I am in control.'

When she came back in, she had his tablets in one hand and a glass of water in the other, but he already seemed a little less stressed.

With shaking hands, he opened the packet and took one out, swallowing it straight away.

Laura stood still for a moment, and then fetched a chair from another desk and brought it over to sit next to him.

'I get panic attacks. I haven't had one in years, not even on the flight over. Don't worry. I'll be fine in a moment.'

She took him at his word and waited, but in her head she called out to God for help.

A moment later, he raised his head and attempted a smile. 'A sausage toasty sounds good. Don't suppose you could put a slice of cheese on mine, could you?'

'I don't know what to do to help you.'

A rush of different emotions came over him. Only Lizzie had cared about him for years. He really wanted Laura to like him, but he didn't want her to feel sorry for him. 'I'm fine, honestly. Breakfast and maybe another coffee will do the trick. Can you give me ten minutes though? I need to call Lizzie.'

Something Carter couldn't quite put his finger on changed in Laura. Like a veil covering her face.

'If you ever want to talk, I'm a very good listener.'

'Thank you.'

'I'll be back shorty with your cheese-smothered sausage toasty!'

She closed the door behind her when she left. Air whooshed out of Carter with a flurry. What was happening to him? He wiped his hands on his jumper and stood up. Maybe he should go home?

He looked at the laptop. His story was flowing, he couldn't give that up. He closed his eyes and did some breathing exercises. 'I am in control. Everything is fine. I am in control. Everything is fine.' Then he took his mobile out of his pocket and called America, totally forgetting about the time difference.

CARTER STRETCHED, LEANING back in his chair. He needed a good run. He missed his running machine. He could feel his muscles protesting at their lack of exercise. He looked out of the window. It hadn't snowed all morning but everything was still covered in snow. Was a run worth the risk of slipping?

He decided it was and went upstairs to get changed.

As soon as he went outside, the cold air nipped at his nose and cheeks. He wanted to run straight away but the path was icy. He crossed the path and went onto the grass. It crunched like broken glass under his feet. The sound was somewhat satisfying. He set off on a slow jog, his common sense telling him a proper run was too risky.

The road through the village had been salted and as it was free of cars he decided to jog on the road. His trainers and the bottom of his tracksuit were soon wet, but he kept on. He felt alive and full of energy. His morning relapse faded from his mind and was replaced by an image of the kind face of the innkeeper's daughter. Such a sweet woman. Such kissable lips!

He ran for about forty minutes down the country lane before turning back toward the village. As he approached the first houses he heard a faint cry that made him grind to a halt. Had he imagined it? He waited a moment to see if he would hear it again. Nothing. He'd just taken two steps when he heard a noise again. He turned and looked at the tiny cottage set back from the road. White-washed walls supported a heavy thatch roof which had at least a foot deep of snow on it. A photograph of the house could easily be put on Christmas cards. He opened the little wooden gate and walked gingerly down the slippery path.

'Help!' The cry was feeble but clear. He raced as fast as he could around the house to where he thought the call was coming from.

Lying on the ground by the side of the house was an old man.

'Oh thank God!' the man said when Carter appeared.

'Are you alright? Silly question, of course you're not. Here let me help you.' Carter bent down and wrapped his arms around the man's chest and helped him sit up.

The man moaned.

'Have you broken anything? Shall I call 911?'

'Grr,' snarled the man. 'Nothing's broken. Think I've twisted my ankle. And flipping rhubarb sticks, what's 911 when it's at home?'

'The emergency services.'

'Where you from? It's 999 in England, and no, I don't want you to call them. I just want you to get me inside!'

'Alright there tiger, calm down! And I'm from New York.' Although the man was downright rude, Carter found himself smiling. 'Let's try again shall we?'

'Huh!'

Carter put his arms around the man again and slowly hauled him upright.

'Arr rhubarb sticks!' the man cried.

'I could try to carry you?'

The man looked at him in shock. 'Certainly not! I've not been carried since I was three years old! Round the back, the front door's locked.'

'OK then, let's see how we get on.'

The man hopped with Carter supporting him and preventing him from going over again on the icy path. Slowly, and with a terrific number of moans and groans, they reached the back door and went into the kitchen.

Once the man was seated on a chair at the table, Carter didn't know what to do. 'Is there anyone I can call to come and help you?'

'I can manage on my own, go on and away with you!'

'I can't leave you like this.'

'I've looked after myself all me life, I don't need anyone now. Now clear off!'

Carter hovered in front of the door. It just didn't feel right to leave him. 'Are you sure there isn't something I can do for you before I go?'

'No!'

Just as Carter put his hand on the handle to open the door, the man changed his mind. 'Wait, I was off out to get some wood for the burner. If you must be a Samaritan then fetch some in for me. You'll find a pile under the lean-to.'

'Sure.'

A minute later, Carter was back in the kitchen his arms full of chopped wood. 'Where do you want it?'

'By fire, in t'other room.'

Carter bent his head to pass through the door into the hallway. The place was dark and cold. He put the wood down next to the hearth and looked around. The man had a bed in the room and a table which still had dinner plates on it. He was obviously living in this room. Carter's heart dropped, he couldn't leave him here, but he could hardly force him to go to hospital either.

He heard a shuffle and turned around. The man had got himself to the doorway and was leaning on the door jamb glaring at him. 'Had a good look did you?'

'I was just coming back.'

'Sure you were.' The man tried hopping into the room.

Carter rushed to his side and took his arm. When he was seated in a high-back chair he asked in a much humbler voice,

'Do you think you could light it for me? I don't think I'd be able to get back up on my own.'

'Of course, though you'll have to guide me, I've never lit a fire in my life.'

'City boys!' But he had a twinkle in his eyes and the slur was accepted in good faith. 'What's your name?'

'Carter. Yours?'

'Joseph Tanner.'

'Nice to meet you, Joseph.'

'Mr Tanner is just fine. You young whippersnappers are all the same, no manners between the lot of yous.'

Joseph gave him step-by-step instructions to light the fire. Carter surprised himself by liking the satisfaction that came when the flames flickered to life.

'Is there anything a rude young whippersnapper can do for you before he leaves?' he asked with a grin.

'Bah! You can make me a pot of tea. You do know how to do *that* don't you?'

'Now there's a funny thing. Up until yesterday I don't think I could have made you one the way you Brits like it, but today I can.'

'Just look around the kitchen, you'll find everything you need there. I have a tray ready with sugar on it. You'll need to fill the milk jug though.' He looked at Carter from under his big, bushy white eyebrows. 'Bah!'

Carter wasn't sure what that meant, but left to attempt the tea.

Ten minutes later, he was back with the tray, complete with tea pot and two mugs.

'Thought you'd gone to China to pick the tea!'

Carter laughed. 'You sure you didn't bang your head when you hit the ground? You seem to have lost your manners. I'm sure people normally say thank you for good deeds.'

Red flushed Joseph's cheeks until he looked like he might burst.

'Shall I play mother?' Carter laughed.

'I never invited you to stay!'

'No, you just asked me to rescue you and then do chores for you.'

'I didn't need rescuing!'

'Really? You mean I should have ignored your yells for help?'

The air deflated out of Joseph and he slumped in his chair.

'Don't rub it in, young man.'

Carter poured them a cup of tea each.

'Three,' said Joseph when Carter reached for the sugar.

'And there's me thinking you're such a sweet man that you don't need sugar!'

'Bah!'

Carter chuckled. After a moment of sitting in silence, Carter asked, 'I see you haven't put up any decorations. Aren't you a fan of Christmas?'

'Well that answer depends on your point of view of Christmas.'

'Mine?'

'Yep.'

'Christmas is about making companies rich. Everything is geared to empty the pockets of normal people. I'm not a Christmas fan. What's your take on it?'

For a moment, Joseph became lost in his thoughts staring at the log fire.

'You gone asleep there, Joseph?'

'Mr Tanner.'

'Mr Tanner.'

'I was remembering Christmases gone by. Times when this house was full of family and laughter. My wife used to be crackers about everything to do with Christmas, from carols to turkey to decorating the tree.' Joseph sighed.

'What about you?'

'I enjoyed watching the joy and fun my family had, but for me Christmas has always been about the birth of Jesus and why He came to Earth.'

Carter, who had been leaning forward in his chair, sat back.

'My favourite verse is in the NIV Bible, John 3:16. For God so loved the world that He gave his one and only son, so that whoever believes in Him shall not perish but have eternal life.'

A chill ran down Carter's back. He'd just known that was what the old man was going to say. He put his cup on the table. 'I best get going. Are you sure you're going to be alright?'

'I'll be reet.'

'Right then, I'll leave you in peace.' He stood up and made his way out of the cottage. I had definitely seen better days. The decorating and furniture revealed that nothing had been done to the house for decades. *My place will be like this one day,* he thought as he shut the door. *Stuck in time, and encased in a sad, forgotten aura.*

As he set off down the road, it struck him that he hadn't hesitated to help Joseph and that he'd put his arms around him without a second thought. He didn't know what on Earth was happening to him.

Any Room at the Inn?

December 20, 2022

'WE CAN'T LEAVE HIM on his own, Dad.'

'He's nothing but a bad tempered old goat. He won't want to come here anyway.'

'Dad!' Laura put her hands on her hips.

To see her so fierce made Carter smile. 'He is hopping around,' he offered.

Laura ignored him. 'We have plenty of room, we're not exactly full!'

'We don't have a lift, he won't be able to get up the stairs,' Bill answered, while vigorously chopping garlic.

'He can have my room. I'll move upstairs until his ankle is better.'

'But your stuff?' Bill finally looked up at her.

'I haven't got that much, Dad. It won't take me long to shift.'

'I can help.'

Both Bill and Laura turned to look at him. He shrugged, 'If you'd like?'

'That would be good, thanks. I'll go and pack up my things and then call you when I'm ready to take them upstairs.'

'I'll wait for you in the quiet room.'

Laura gave him a soft smile and turned back to Bill. 'It'll just be for a couple of days.'

Bill shrugged. 'It's your room. If you're happy, I'm happy. And truth be told I canna say no to ya girl.'

'Thanks, Dad.' She wrapped her arms around his middle and squeezed tight.

'There's one good thing,' said Bill when she let go.

'What's that?'

'He's not like a dog you'll want to keep forever! I'm sure you're going to be reet happy when he goes home!'

Laura laughed. 'Aye, 'tis true that!'

It took a couple of hours to empty the room and put fresh linen in. Laura's cheeks radiated a rosy heat by the time they'd finished. 'I don't know what I would have done without your help.'

'No problem. Are you ready to fetch the old misery guts?'

'Ready as I'll ever be. He'll probably put up a fight you know. He won't want to come. We'll have to use our best powers of persuasion.'

'I don't know if I would have much sway with him. I think he took an instant dislike to me!'

'Oh, never mind him. He dislikes everyone!'

They went in Carter's Wrangler.

'I see your car is back in the car park.'

'Yeah, Dad walked down with a jerry can of petrol and fetched it back as soon as the gritters had salted the road.'

'Luckily you were close to home.'

'My guardian angel always looks after me.'

Carter tried not to react, but inside him a storm brewed. All the mentions of God since his trip started had set him on the path of memories. Now, as he drove along the slush-filled lane, images of his adoptive parents came to mind. His stomach twisted. He hadn't returned their love or offers of affection. Guilt over the way he'd left them washed over him.

He shook his head to clear the images and concentrate on the road.

'Are you OK?'

'Yep.'

When he didn't say any more Laura returned her gaze to the front.

'How'doo Joseph?' Laura called as she opened the door, after a good hard knock.

'That you, Laura?'

'Aye, can I come in?'

'Sure, you know the way. Be quick and shut door before all the warmth be gone!'

When they appeared in the living room, Joseph snarled, 'What you bring that pesky foreigner for!'

'We've come to take you back to the pub. You can stay with us for a couple of days until your ankle mends.'

Laura had expected him to argue, but his body slumped like a deflating balloon. 'That be reet good of yous.'

Laura blinked a couple of times, for a moment lost for words. 'Can I fetch some of your clothes for you? Are they in drawers upstairs?'

He pointed to the ironing board that stood alongside the wall. It was piled high with folded clothes. 'All me stuff's there.'

'Do you have a bag?'

'Just those plastic ones hanging off the door handle.'

Laura pulled a few plastic shopping bags out of the bag on the door and began to fill them with some of his clothes.

'If you want to be useful ya can fetch the stuff out of the fridge,' he said looking at Carter.

'Sure thing.'

'Take a bag with 'ee. There's a ham in there, and milk and cheese. Bring it all, twill only go off if I leave it 'ere.'

Carter left them and went into the kitchen. Although the house seemed to be piled with too much stuff and Joseph obviously only lived in the downstairs part, everything was fresh and clean. After emptying the fridge of anything he thought might go off, he went back into the living room.

Carter pointed to the fire. 'Do we need to put it out?'

'No, just put the guard in front of it will you. It will die down slowly on its own.'

Carter placed the fireguard in front of the burning logs, which had already nearly burned out.

'Pass us me coat, lad,' said Joseph pointing to the coat on the back of the chair opposite him. Carter held it for him as Joseph stood up and shoved his arms through the sleeves. 'Ta.'

Carter held onto one arm and Laura took the other as Joseph hopped his way out of the cottage.

Once Joseph's things had been set up in his room, they escorted him to the bar and got him comfortable in his favourite armchair by the fire.

Bill came over. 'How'doo old man?'

'Be much better with a whiskey in me hand!'

'To be clear, Laura has given you her room and I don't mind sharing my meals with you, but anything from the bar you're going to have to cough up the pennies.'

'Eee, and they say Christmas is the season for generosity. We could do with some of that cheer in 'ere!'

Carter opened his mouth to speak, an obvious rebuke forming on his lips. Laura put a hand on his arm and shook her head.

'And they say manners are dead, people ought to pay us a visit to know even our over-the-hill members still remember them! Apple pies, Joseph, you do test a man you do.'

Then they burst out laughing. Bill tapped him on the shoulder. 'Be back with your drink in a jiffy.'

'Have you been introduced to Sharon yet?'

Carter glanced down at Laura. Her eyes sparkled and brimmed with life. Why did his heart suddenly feel so light? 'No.'

'Come on.'

Carter followed Laura over to the bar. A comely red-head stood on the other side of the bar pulling a pint for a short ruddy-faced man in a flat cap.

'Sharon, this is our Christmas guest, Carter Johnson. Carter this is Sharon.'

Carter raised his hand and gave it a little shake. 'How do you do?'

She grinned as she handed the full and frothy-headed beer glass to the customer. 'Your Olive will have something to say if you stay 'ere too long, Noah.'

'She can have a chat with 'erself, she can, but me old ears 'ave long been shut up to nagging.'

Sharon turned to face Carter and Laura. 'I'm very well, thank you. And how are you?'

He could tell by her lilting tone that this might be a bit too formal for her.

Laura took pity on his sudden discomfort. 'Sharon has worked for us ever since we opened. We'd be lost without her, she's a marvel.'

'Aye, you're too kind, Laura.'

'Not at all,' said Bill. 'We couldn't manage without you.'

Carter caught the look Sharon gave Bill and knew instantly that she loved him. Bill nodded and went over to Joseph with the whiskey without seemingly noticing. Could the man not know?

He caught Laura smiling at him. 'Not very bright my Dad!'

'Oy you!' Sharon gave Laura a playful nudge. 'He has his reasons for not noticing me, you leave 'im be. Can I get you a drink, Carter?'

'Decaffeinated coffee would be good, if you have any?'

'I'll get it.' Laura went behind the bar and into the kitchen.

'You're staying with us for a while, I hear.'

Carter sat down on a bar stool. He liked this woman, from her round rosy cheeks to her gentle speech to her flaming locks, she oozed warmth. 'Yes a few weeks. I had planned to go walking every day but I wasn't expecting this weather.'

'We haven't had it this cold at this time of year since 2018. And it doesn't normally snow around here this heavily either, so you're unlucky with your timing.'

But if he'd come another year Laura might not have been here, so bad weather or not, he couldn't help being glad he was here now.

Laura soon returned with his coffee. 'By the way it's quiz night and Dad's made a hotpot for the customers. Would you like to eat in here tonight with everyone, or would you prefer to look at the menu?'

'What's hotpot?'

Sharon put her elbow on the bar, eager to educate the American guest. 'Stewed lamb and carrots topped with sliced potatoes and baked in the oven. We serve it with pickled red cabbage. 'Tis proper winter bait, so it is. Ya canna go home without tryin' it.'

'Well, I guess I'd better have some then!' laughed Carter.

Sharon slapped his shoulder. 'Reet choice! You'll be brossen after all that scran!'

Carter turned to Laura, his expression crying for help. She laughed. 'You made the right choice, and you'll be full once you've finished the meal.'

'Oh!'

Just then Mykyta and Ivanna came running into the room. 'Not fair,' declared Ivanna with a downturned mouth.

'What's not?' asked Laura.

'No school!' Ivanna had obviously been crying, her face still red and blotchy.

Laura took a tissue and wiped Ivanna's tears away. 'It's safer to stay at home.'

Anna came rushing in. She put a hand on each of the children's shoulders. 'Sorry to bother.' She started propelling them out of the bar.

'Anna, let them stay,' said Bill coming over. 'We'll be serving dinner in here tonight anyway. Let them pick a table to play games at. Hey you,' he suddenly noticed Ivanna's face. 'What's up?'

'She was going to be Mary in the school nativity, but now the school has closed early they won't be doing it,' said Anna.

'Now that's a reet shame.' Bill hunched down to be face-level with Ivanna. 'How would you like to decorate a Christmas tree instead?'

Laura gasped. Bill turned and smiled at her. ''Bout time, aye what you say?'

'I think it's a really good idea, Dad.'

'Right then,' Bill stood up. 'First thing tomorrow we'll go out and find us a tree, and then we'll decorate the whole pub, just like old times.'

Laura threw her arms around her dad.

Bill kissed the top of her head. 'Be alright, love. We'll not forget her, but it's time to celebrate once more.'

Bill looked over the top of Laura's head at Carter. 'I'm sorry, I know we said that we didn't celebrate Christmas, and we haven't done for a few years...'

'It's fine,' said Carter. 'Really it is. I understand.'

When Laura pulled away her eyes were brimming over, she gave them a hasty wipe and turned to smile at Carter. 'Thank you,' she said.

'Now you two,' said Bill turning to look at the kids. 'Have you met our American guest?'

They shook their heads.

'Carter, this is Ivanna and Mike. It's not his name but for the life of me I can't pronounce it properly so they've given me permission to call him Mike.'

'It's very nice to meet you,' said Carter offering Mykyta his hand first.

Mykyta shook it. 'Are you rich? Mum tell, you very big…' he asked his mum something in Ukrainian.

'Author,' she answered in English.

'Author!' he declared with a grin.

Laura answered before Carter could. 'We don't normally ask questions like that, Mike. Most people like to keep things private.'

'It's fine,' cut in Carter. 'I used to have more money than I do now, but my books haven't been doing very well recently so I'm not as rich as I used to be.' He offered his hand to shake hands with Ivanna. She hid behind her mother and peeped at him from under Anna's arm.

Carter dropped his hand and offered a smile instead. 'It's nice to meet you Ivanna.'

She gave him a timid smile and then completely hid behind Anna.

'Stay with us Anna.' Bill touched her arm. 'There is a pile of board games on the dresser over there. Pick a table near the fire and make yourself at home.'

At first it looked like she might refuse, but then as she took in Mykyta's expectant face she changed her mind and gave a short nod. Mykyta instantly ran off to the cupboards to check out the games. 'I will stay with them a while and then come to help, no.'

'Only if they are happy without you in here, otherwise we can manage.'

'Thank you, Bill.' Anna took Ivanna's hand and they went over to join Mykyta.

'I'm happy to help,' said Carter surprising himself. He had planned to go back to writing.

'An extra pair of hands is always appreciated,' said Laura. 'Let's start by putting the plates in the warmer.'

He followed her into the kitchen. She went straight to the sink to wash her hands so he did the same. He studied her face while they dried their hands. She had a straight nose and a wide mouth, her skin was flawless. She really was a beauty. Yet it was the kindness in her eyes that drew him in. He'd known her such a short time and yet he had a longing to love her and become part of her world. The thought shocked him. His world really was topsy-turvy at the moment.

'Are you alright?' Her face was full of concern. How long had he been lost in his thoughts?

'I wonder if I might help with the decorations tomorrow?'

'Why of course you can.'

'What time will you start?'

'Probably about eleven. I assume we're going over to Sheldon Farm for the tree. Have you ever cut down your own tree?'

'I've never had a tree.'

'What? Not even when you were little?'

He was just about to say no, thinking of the Christmases with his real mum, but then he recalled the festivities with his adoptive parents, Julie and Daniel. He'd spent way more years with them as opposed to the six he'd spent with his birth mother. Why did he always squash memories of them? Since arriving in England, memories of them had come to his mind like popping corn. Maybe being close to another family had ignited them.

'I never helped put the decorations up. My parents always tried to involve me but I was a terrible loner and preferred to lock myself in my room with my books.'

'Escapism.'

'Exactly!'

Her eyes swam with kindness. 'Well, they do say there is a first time for everything.'

'They do.'

They started filling the warmer with plates. Under her breath Laura said, 'I'm glad that you want to decorate with us this year.'

Warmth spread throughout his body. 'So am I.'

LATER THAT NIGHT, Carter lay on his back staring at the ceiling. Over the years he hadn't given much thought to Julie and Daniel. Since arriving in England they'd never been far from his thoughts. He'd treated them badly, he'd always known that, yet it was only now that it bothered him. Not that he'd ever been nasty to them, but he knew his distance and indifference had always hurt them. The time had come for him to right that wrong. When the right moment presented itself he would give them a call. The thought of it churned his stomach. Maybe too much time had passed? Maybe it would be better to let sleeping dogs lie? Yet even as he pondered on it, he knew he had to call.

He closed his eyes. A pretty face with loving eyes floated before him. *Could someone as lovely as Laura fall in love with a Grinch like me?*

Where's the Wise Men?

December 21, 2022

'DAD, I'VE HAD AN IDEA!'

'What's that?'

'I think we should put on a nativity here at the pub!'

'Really? When? How you goin' pull that off?'

'I've been thinking about it since the moment I got up. There's Emily, Hyacinth, Maeve, and Martha, and I thought even Ted might want to put his theatrical expertise into practice one more time! If we all pull together I'm sure we can do something for the children.'

Bill put his hands on either side of Laura's head and pulled her forward to place a kiss on her forehead. 'If anyone can pull this off, Love, then it's you. You go for it!'

'Great! I think we should do it on Christmas Eve, at about three o'clock. Here, if that's OK? It's just the church is so cold and will take too much money to warm it up. Plus I don't know how many people will come anyway.'

'It's fine Laura, whatever you think best. If you're inviting people to come and watch it, I could put on a buffet. We could ask people for donations to send to the relief organizations in Ukraine. What do you think?'

'Oh that's a great idea! Right, I'm going to go to my room and start calling around, see who and what I can drum up.'

An hour later, Laura was buzzing. Before starting the calls, she had clasped her hands together and poured out prayers of thanks followed by a request for the Lord to bless her plans and if He was in agreement then everything would fall neatly into place.

Every person she had called had been happy to help. Emily had tried to convince her to hold it in the church, but Laura just had a feeling that it should be in the pub and eventually Emily had agreed. She would search the church store room and bring over the nativity scenery that hadn't been used in years. She didn't know how much was still usable but she would bring over whatever was good enough.

Maeve and Martha had put her on loudspeaker and had both spoken at the same time in a rush. Laughing, Laura had to ask them to speak one at a time. They both agreed to help sew some costumes, as it happened they had some old threadbare sheets that would be perfect for cutting up. They would bring their sewing machine and bits and pieces and be with Laura within the hour.

There were just two people left to call.

At first, Hyacinth had been very quiet and showed no enthusiasm for helping.

'If you can't help us, Hyacinth, that's fine. You mustn't worry about it.'

'Can we have carol singers?'

'What?'

'I've been knitting red hats. I thought the Lord told me to knit twelve for a carol service this year. I mean, I was flummoxed at first. We haven't had a carol service in Berrycombe for over ten years. On Sunday mornings now, as you know, there are what... about twelve of us on a good day? So I thought to myself I must have misheard the Lord. But this nagging feeling wouldn't go away, so for the last couple of weeks I've been knitting every evening and today I've just finished the twelfth one.'

'I don't know if I can find people to sing, Hyacinth.'

A sigh came down the phone.

Laura was a people-pleaser, she knew that. She always tried to make sure everyone was happy. Quite an impossible task, but one she persisted in. Her dad would tell her off now, for she spoke without too much thought.

'You know what... I know at least six people who are feeling very festive, so all I need to do is find another six. Who cares what we sound like? We just need to praise the birth of Christ; we don't need to be professionals.'

'Oh! Laura you are a sweetheart. I'll gather up my things and be with you shortly.'

Laura stared at the phone. Decorations, a nativity and now carol singers... and there were only four days left to Christmas Eve. Maybe she was biting off more than she could chew?

'Hi Ted, how you doing?'

'Is that you, Laura?'

'Yes. I confess I'm calling because I'm greatly in need of your skills.'

'Really? What's going on?'

'Could you come to the pub and help us put on a nativity?'

Ted burst out laughing and Laura's heart sank. She'd kind of been banking on his help.

When she didn't respond, Ted stopped laughing. 'Are you serious?'

'Ivanna was going to be Mary in the school nativity and she's heartbroken because the school has closed early and now she won't be in it. She wanted Anna to film it and send it to her dad.' Laura crossed her fingers. There was nothing quite like a little emotional blackmail to prompt people into action, but she felt guilty for doing it.

'How many people will be in my production?'

Laura grinned from ear to ear and tilted her head back and mouthed 'thank you' at the ceiling. 'Honestly I don't know yet, I'm still gathering everyone in. Will you help us then?'

'I'll be at the pub in twenty minutes!'

'Thank you Ted, thank you, thank you, thank you! No one could throw a last-minute show together like you.'

'OK girl, less of the flattery you had me at the emotional blackmail moment.'

'Oops, sorry.'

'Don't be. I'm sixty-nine and for the last ten months every time I've watched the news about what's happening in Ukraine I've started crying. So, if I can help two children enjoy their Christmas just a tiny bit, I'm there. You've got me.' His voice was breaking up and even Laura felt the tears on the rise.

'Thank you, Ted. Drive carefully and see you soon.'

Now she just had to find out if she could encourage some more children to take part.

'Hi Joanne, how are you?'

'Hi Laura, we're OK ta. How about you?'

'I'm fine, thanks. I was wondering if Matthew would like to take part in an impromptu nativity we're putting on at the pub? I know it's short notice but everyone is on their way over now to see what we can do. I'd love it if you would like to help and if Matthew wanted to take part.'

'Let me ask him, hold on a minute.'

Laura could hear a muffled conversation between mother and son. A moment later, Joanne was back. 'Yes, we're in. Did you say you're starting right now?'

'Yes! No time to lose, lol. We're hoping to put it on Christmas Eve in the afternoon. Dad's also doing a donation dinner to raise money for Ukraine, but we don't expect people to put anything in, it's only if they have a pound or two spare.'

'We'll be with you as soon as we can. Did you know that Baldwins have their grandchildren with them for Christmas? You might want to give them a call. I know the Jones and the Browns have gone away this year, so I don't know of any more children around.'

'That's great, thanks Joanne. See you soon!'

A short call to the Baldwin farm confirmed that the whole family would come to watch the nativity and stay for supper, but that the children didn't want to participate.

'Three children, Dad! How can we put on a nativity with only three?'

'You know at the birth, there was in fact only one child?'

'Yes, but...'

'No buts, girl. You've started this nativity now. You have a Mary and a Joseph, and Matthew could be a shepherd. You need to find three adults to be wise men. Where you'll find three wise men in Berrycombe I have no idea!' He stopped to chuckle at his own joke. 'But you'll find them. Go get 'em, girl.'

'I can't imagine any men wanting to take part in a nativity, Dad.'

'You never know until you ask. What about Carter?'

'Don't be daft, I can't ask him.'

'Why not? He's very sweet on you. I'm sure he'll do anything to get in your good books.'

'Dad! He isn't.'

'I think he is.'

'I *know* he isn't. He's got someone back home called Lizzie.'

'Oh, I didn't know that. What a pity. I was sure he was falling for you.'

Laura's face dropped. If she was honest she'd kind of been falling for him until she realized he had someone already.

'Arr love.' Bill came from behind the bar and pulled her into a hug. 'There's someone special out there for you, I know there is.'

'OK, OK,' Laura pulled herself away. 'I've got a show to put on!'

'That's my girl!' Bill cuffed her gently on the chin.

One by one, cars started pulling into the car park. Before long the pub was a hive of noise and activity. Everyone was chatting ten to the dozen and for the first time since her mum died, Laura felt a rush of Christmas spirit. A lump kept forming in her throat which she constantly drowned with a glass of water. She didn't have time for tears, not even happy ones!

The last to arrive (of course) was Ted. His flower-covered Beetle pulled through the gates with a loud toot-toot.

At sixty-nine, Ted oozed as much charisma as he'd done when he was twenty-one and quite the man-about-town. A sixties fanatic he walked into the pub as if he'd just stepped out of an old film. His hair, although now grey, fell in curled tresses that were still thick and bouncy, held in place by a multi-coloured headband.

'Hellooooo everyone,' he said with a flourish as he swooped in. 'Soooo, a nativity, totally groovy.'

Everyone groaned.

'Laura!'

Laura jumped and turned around to look at him.

'What's wrong with this place? Where are the tree and the decorations?'

'It's on the agenda for this afternoon.'

'Right, thank goodness for that. This place is totally lacking any atmosphere, my dear. Gather around, let's get this meeting off the ground.'

They pulled tables and chairs together and had a 'show and trimmings' meeting.

'What do you mean we've only got three actors? That's just impossible. I'm a miracle worker, I know,' he paused to smile at his own flattery, 'but even I need a cast to work with.'

'If I don't have to speak, I'll be a wise man,' said Sharon.

Joseph snorted. 'Not to be too obvious, but you're a woman!'

'Does it matter?' asked Laura.

'Women and men have swapped parts in pantomimes for donkey years,' Ted waved his arms around.

'This is a nativity!' barked Joseph.

'Well, that makes you the first volunteer then,' said Ted, 'now we just need two more.'

'I can't be a wise man!'

'Of course you can,' said Ted.

'I can hardly walk!'

'I'm sure the wise men could hardly walk after the distance they travelled. Now suggestions everyone! Who else could be a wise man?'

Different names were proposed.

'Right Hyacinth, that's agreed. You go and do some calling and use your best persuasion to get them here tomorrow for our one-and-only rehearsal. If they can't do it we'll need a miracle.'

Hyacinth left with a few names. The rest of them tried to work out the costumes and props needed. She returned after ten minutes. All the men suggested had either gone away for the holiday or didn't want to be in the play. Of those remaining in Berrycombe, all said they would come on the day though to support the event. 'Brian wants to help though. He'll come on Christmas Eve and help set up.'

'I think we need an angel,' said Maeve.

Ted groaned. 'We don't have any more children!'

Emily sat up making herself taller. 'I don't mind playing an angel!

Ted wrote her name down on his list. 'Very well.'

Just as Laura thought it was all coming together, Ted dropped a bombshell.

'We can't do the nativity to *that* music!' Maeve went rigid she was so indignant.

'Maeve, sweetheart, go away and listen to the words. I'm telling you, in between the Bible verses these are the songs we're going to sing. The whole thing should be over in half an hour to forty-five minutes. You can't hold children's attention longer than that. These songs will keep everyone attentive. Trust me!'

'But I love singing carols.' Maeve's chin wobbled, making the bun on the top of her head wobble too.

'As it happens,' said Laura placing her hand over Maeve's icy vein-covered hand. 'Hyacinth has requested we gather twelve carol singers.'

'Twelve! How are you going to do that?'

'How many here are happy to sing with me?' asked Laura.

Everyone raised their hands.

'There, that's eight already. I'm going to ask Dad, so that's nine. We just need three more and I'm sure we'll find them.'

'You know Elmer had an amazing singing voice in the day. I bet he could still sing a tune if we asked him,' said Martha.

'He did, didn't he,' said Ted. 'I remember he used to sing at everyone's wedding.'

'And their funerals!' added Joseph.

'Joseph!' called several people at once.

'It's the truth!'

'We just need two more then,' said Laura. I'll ring around all the farms and see if anyone can join us.'

'When will we rehearse?' asked Maeve.

'How about each evening at seven, until Christmas Eve?'

'That's only three times?' said Maeve chewing her lip.

Laura tapped on the table. 'Listen everyone, the whole thing has disaster written all over it. But you know what… it doesn't matter. We don't need to look or sound good. We just need to celebrate Jesus's birth, cheer up the children and hopefully make a bit of money to send to Ukraine.'

Tree of Love

December 21, 2022

AFTER THE HECTIC MEETING, Laura enjoyed the peaceful drive over to Sheldon Farm.

'You're quiet,' said Carter not taking his eyes off the road.

'Just taking a minute. Have you ever started something in good faith and then thought that maybe you're just crazy for doing so?'

Carter laughed. 'No, I can honestly say I've never done that.'

Laura sighed. 'I think I may have bitten off more than I can chew.'

Carter reached over with his left hand and touched her hand for a brief moment before returning it to the wheel. 'Everything's going to be just fine.'

'I hope so. I only meant to cheer the children up. Somehow it's been like a snowball that just keeps growing and growing. I don't suppose you'd be a wise man, would you?'

'All the wisdom I have is yours simply ask.'

'No,' Laura chuckled. 'I mean literally, we still need two wise men for the nativity.'

'Oh, I don't think so. I don't do people most of the time. I definitely can't participate in a play.'

'You don't have to say anything. Ted says he will narrate the whole thing so no one has to learn lines. You just need to put a cardboard crown on your head and pretend to be a king from the East!'

'Would it help you out?'

'Absolutely!'

'Then I'll do it.'

Laura spun in the seat to look at him. 'Really?'

'Sure, you just want me to follow the other wise men, right? Walk down to a crib and that's it?'

'Yes, that's it completely, and maybe help Joseph along.'

'Joseph's going to be a wise man!'

'Uh, huh.'

Carter barked a short laugh. 'OK then, I'm in.'

'Oh, I could kiss you!'

Carter turned his head slightly to look at her. A smile danced upon his lips. 'I think I would like that.'

Heat flamed Laura's cheeks. 'No, I mean, I wasn't being serious, it's a saying when you're happy, I would never kiss you... I mean put you in *that* position!'

Carter noticed her red cheeks and flustered face and took it to mean she was absolutely not attracted to him. His insides flipped, as disappointment rose like a bitter taste in his mouth.

A short time later, they pulled into the farm.

Mark Sheldon came out of the farmhouse dressed for arctic weather. 'How'doo,' he called as he approached the car.

'Reet fine Mark, thanks. How's your lot? Are you ready for the big day?'

'Just about, Sue's cooking up a storm and Bobby helped me put up a tree yesterday. Not doing presents this year, what with times being as tight as they are, so I guess we're done.'

'Did many people come for trees this year?' Laura's face showed her concern. A lot of families had already left Berrycombe, their homes being snapped up by people wanting holiday homes. It hurt to see her world change the way it had.

'You're the only one, lass. Been a bad year all round.'

'Didn't you sell any to the shops in Kendal?'

'No, some big supplier offered impossibly cheap prices. There was no point me cutting any down. Any road, let's get going and find you a tree for the pub. No charge... and before you start to argue,' he lifted his finger to silence Laura. 'Your dad has been good to us over the years and we appreciate he still buys his fresh vegetables and eggs from us. This tree is our gift to you.'

'Thank you Mark that's very generous of you.'

'Let's go on the tractor, it'll get us there quicker than foot.'

They climbed aboard and Laura sighed in relief to be out of the biting wind. 'Have you heard the forecast?'

'Aye, 'tis not looking good is it?'

'No. The cold front is lingering for at least the next eight or nine days. It's going to start snowing again this evening.'

'Don't think we've had a Christmas like this for nigh on fifteen years. Are you stocked up with logs at the pub?'

'Yes. Dad's also just had another delivery of oil for the Aga, so we'll be toasty.'

'What's an Aga?' asked Carter.

'It's a cooker in the kitchen. We use it for cooking, but it also heats the kitchen and that part of the building. It's never turned off so it costs quite a lot of money, but we just love it.'

'Hey Mark, I don't suppose you'd be a wise man for us in our nativity, would you? Joseph is one, and Carter here is the second. You don't have to say anything Ted's going to narrate.'

'I don't have to say anything?'

'No,' Laura chuckled, 'just wear a cardboard crown, carry a gift and lay it by the crib – which hopefully, Emily will have cleaned up. Ah that reminds me, you wouldn't happen to have a handful of hay we could have for the crib would you?'

Mark burst out laughing. 'How long is this list going to get?'

'That's it, promise.'

'You know what… I'd love to be a king so long as you don't want me to talk or sing.'

'Ah… about singing, we're starting a choi…'

'Absolutely not! But Sue's got a reet fine voice; you should ask her on the way back.'

'Will do.'

They drove for about fifteen minutes until they came to the edge of the fir woodlands that Mark had planted twelve years ago. This was supposed to have been the second year of making a profit. Hopefully next year would see England out of the recession, before all the farms were lost.

'Have a walk through, pick any one you want.'

Carter and Laura jumped off the tractor and set off amongst the firs. Snow lay on the branches presenting a stunning winter wonderland. Mark followed a little behind with a cordless saw.

'We just need to have carollers singing in the background and you'd have the classical Christmas image,' said Carter, fighting back the urge to take hold of Laura's hand.

'Good King Wenceslas looked out on the Feast of Stephen

When the snow lay round about, deep and crisp and even

Brightly shone the moon that night, though the frost was cruel

When a poor man came in sight, gathering winter fu-u-el.'

'Wow, I mean wow Laura! You should be on the stage or something.'

Laura gave a shy smile and returned to searching for a tree.

Carter hurried to walk beside her, 'Seriously, haven't you ever thought about a singing career?'

'We all thought our Laura would make it on the stage, but she gave it up to stay with her dad, bless her bones,' answered Mark. 'We all went to see her in London's West End once, she was amazing.'

'I was only in the chorus.'

'Shone like a star you did, put the rest to shame!'

'It was a long time ago, and he's exaggerating!' Laura rolled her eyes. She suddenly stopped walking. 'Oh! It's got to be this one! Mark can we take this one?'

In front of them, about seven feet tall and full of thick branches, stood an ideal fir. Laura put her gloved hands up to her mouth. 'It's perfect,' she whispered.

'Then it's the one for you.' Mark took the safety cover off the saw and set to work cutting it down. 'Here,' he said to Carter when he'd finished, 'help with this please.'

They started at the bottom and pulled netting over it to hold the branches in. They lifted an end each and set off back to the tractor.

'Come on in and have a chat with our Sue about the singing,' said Mark when they arrived back at the farm.

Sue didn't hesitate. 'I'd love to join you. Seven o'clock tonight you say?'

'Yes, seven in the pub. Thanks so much Sue be lovely to have you with us.'

Mark grimaced. 'You'll need as many good singers as you can get to drown out Emily's whining!'

'Arr, don't tease. Her heart is in the right place,' said Laura.

'Shame her voice doesn't match the sweetness of her personality!'

'Mark!' Sue nudged him with her elbow.

'Yikes, bitter turnips! Not so hard, love.'

'Don't you listen to him, Laura. When we sing altogether she'll blend in marvellously.'

'Hopefully!' Mark nodded his head several times like a yoyo, putting his all into stressing his doubts.

'What's wrong with Emily's singing?' asked Carter.

The others laughed and groaned. 'Imagine nails being scratched down a chalkboard, and then add such high notes as to break glass!' said Mark.

'Oh, she's not *that* bad!' said Laura.

'Will you stay for a Baileys or a coffee?' asked Sue.

'No ta, we should get back. We need to decorate the pub before we have the choir practice. It's all go-go-go!'

'See you tonight, then.'

They flattened the back seats of the Wrangler but still had to tie the boot door down with string allowing the tree to poke out. Before long, they'd returned and were hefting the tree inside.

Bill and Sharon had been hard at it since they'd left. The three children, Anna, Joanne, Maeve and Martha were happily encamped at a table in the corner making strings of paper chains while singing along with the carols that were coming out of the CD player.

Bill was blowing up balloons and Sharon was draping tinsel over the stairs bannisters.

Laura's heart swelled with happiness.

Carter looked at her glistening eyes and longed to lean forward and kiss her. He pulled himself up straight. 'Right, where are we putting this monster?'

Bill pointed to the corner of the room. 'To the right of the fireplace. I've put a bucket of soil there for you to stand it in.'

Laura helped carry the tree across the room. 'Did you find the box of tree decorations, Dad?'

'Yes, love. It's by the fireplace waiting for you.'

As soon as the tree was up and the netting cut, Laura rushed to the box and rifled through it. She pulled out an angel that had seen better days. 'Can you put this on the top for me?'

He didn't say anything, but Carter's raised eyebrows shouted 'really?'

'It was my mum's when she was a little girl.'

Carter raised it up and carefully positioned it on the topmost point.

'You should do that last you know,' Bill called, taking a breather from blowing up balloons. 'You know when you put the lights on it'll probably wobble and fall.'

'We'll be careful,' said Carter.

'Are you sure you wouldn't rather be writing?' asked Laura.

'I'm exactly where I want to be.'

The two of them locked eyes and the rest of the room faded away. The connection between them so strong, that happiness trembled inside her.

'Laura, Laura!' Ivanna pulled on her sleeve.

The precious moment faded. Laura grinned down at the young girl. 'What is it?'

'Can you help me hang these?' She lifted a long stream of a paper chain.

'Why don't I do that, while you get on with the tree?' said Carter.

The next two hours flew by. The pub, although full of people, saw no one buying anything from the bar. Everyone took part and helped transform the main bar room into a Christmas delight. Even grumpy-drawers Joseph couldn't help participating and even laughed once or twice.

'Just one last thing,' said Laura before rushing out of the lounge. She returned shortly with shoe box that had been covered in Christmas wrapping paper.

'What's that?' asked Carter.

'Inside are pieces of plain card and little envelopes which have holes in them for ribbon. We each take a piece of card and write something on it. Then we put it in an envelope, thread a piece of red ribbon through the hole, and then tie it to a branch on the tree.'

'The idea,' said Sharon 'is to write something encouraging for whoever opens the envelope.'

Bill pulled up next to them and sat down on a bar stool. He took a piece of card, an envelope and a piece of red ribbon out of the box. 'We don't know who will pick our cards, so we need to write something that will encourage the reader whoever they are, whether male or female, child or adult.'

'What kind of things do you write?' asked Carter.

'Whatever comes to mind,' replied Laura.

Bill picked up a pen. 'It could be a line from a poem, a verse from the Bible, or it could just say something encouraging like... you are loved. It really is up to you, but you mustn't let anyone know what you've written and you don't write anything on the envelope so no one knows who is picking what.'

'We do it instead of buying presents,' explained Laura. 'Most of us in the village have been struggling in the last few years so we created this gift idea. For the last two years we hung the envelopes on a piece of string on the wall, but Sharon and I thought it would be nice if we put them on the tree this year.'

'We'll start it off,' said Bill, 'and as new people arrive up until Christmas Day, we'll invite them to write one as well. We'll each pick one off the tree in the afternoon after our Christmas dinner.'

The group dispersed into different parts of the room to write on the cards, including the children. Then one-by-one everyone took their envelopes and tied them to a branch on the tree.

Carter was stuck for a little while, not knowing what to write. Then he remembered a quote from the book Annette White wrote about bucket lists. He scribbled down, *Believe that you can and you will.* He popped the card inside the envelope and went to hang it on the tree.

CARTER SURPRISED EVERYONE when he came to the choir practice and played the piano for them. Laura thought Emily might protest as she played the organ in church, but she announced her arthritic fingers were more than grateful to not have to play.

After the rehearsal when everyone was having a drink before going home, Laura sent up a prayer of thanks to the Lord. Today had been a pure joy and as far as she was concerned a little miracle had just taken place. Not only had Bill agreed to decorate the pub, but just now, when he'd been standing *very* close to Sharon, Laura had caught the moment when his hand had brushed slowly across Sharon's for no reason as they smiled at each other.

'At last,' she whispered under her breath.

Oh Ms Appleby!

December 22, 2022

'THERE'S SOMETHING I'VE BEEN meaning to ask.' Carter took a bite of toast.

Laura looked over the table at him. 'What's that?'

He finished his mouthful. 'What is it with all the mentions of fruit and vegetables?'

'Be more specific.' However, there was a glint in her eye that made Carter think she knew exactly what he was on about.

'Like yesterday, when Sue nudged Mark he said something about turnips. And there's Joseph who has a thing for rhubarb – what's that all about?'

Laura grinned. 'OK I'll tell you. Nearly four hundred years ago, Oliver Cromwell appointed himself Lord Protector of the Commonwealth. It was in December in 1653. He set down very strict rules on how to live. One of the laws he passed was against swearing. If you were caught swearing you received a fine, if you did so more than once you could be sent to prison. Obviously, over time everyone forgot about him and eventually the law was abolished. But in 1920 a vicar was appointed to Berrycombe who was very opposed to bad language. He introduced a swear box in church and anyone heard swearing near him was expected to put a day's wage into the box. People very quickly became careful about their speech. You still with me?'

'Sure am, it's fascinating.' He munched on his toast.

'Some of the farmers got together one Sunday after church, and decided there are just moments in life when an emphasis is definitely needed to reveal how upset you are. So… they introduced a fruit and vegetable way of swearing. They could declare the words as much as they wanted, everyone knew what they meant but the vicar couldn't ask them for a day's wage.'

'Ingenious! I think I'll have to give it a go. Are there any rules?'

'Not really, but for politeness sake we don't use something already being used. Anything else goes.'

'I wonder what I could say?'

'Something will come to mind.'

'I'll give it some thought and try it out on you later. I haven't heard you say anything yet. Do you have one?'

'I try not to get that upset that I need one, but I have been heard to say 'carrot tops' once or twice.'

'That suits you!'

Laura bowed her head slightly. 'Thank you.'

'So what's on the agenda for today, besides choir at seven?'

'Shouldn't you be writing?'

'I was writing until two this morning. I'm ready to do something else right now. I'll probably try and write again after lunch, but this morning I'm all yours.'

When Laura smiled, dimples appeared in her cheeks. Carter thought them totally adorable. In fact, each day Laura herself became more and more adorable. He couldn't take his eyes off her!

'We have the rehearsal at eleven, and before that I wanted to go and pick some pine branches and holly. I'm going to make a wreath to go on the mantel over the fireplace.'

'Right, I'll go get wrapped up and come with you... if that's OK with you?'

'Sure, it will be nice to have company. Meet you by the front door in say... fifteen minutes?'

'That works for me.'

Laura cleared away the breakfast things. Carter downed his coffee and went upstairs to get dressed.

'You know, love, maybe you should put a bit of distance between you two seeing as he's spoken for already?'

Laura looked at Bill and slapped her hands onto her hips. 'Dad! We're not doing anything wrong. We're just going to gather some greenery to finish the decorating. *Nothing* else!'

'Just guard your heart, love, that's all.'

'I will. I always do.'

The look on Bill's face said he didn't think she did.

Laura tutted and went to put her coat and Wellington boots on.

'Ready,' called Carter bounding down the stairs.

Laura couldn't help grinning. He looked as excited as a young boy. 'We just need to pop into the shed to get a couple of baskets and some secateurs.'

'Banana skins! I thought we'd be going straight out.'

Laura lowered her chin, looking at him side-on she shook her head.

'Not bananas?'

For an answer she pulled her woolly hat further down and shook her head again.

Once the two wicker trugs had been fetched from the shed, they walked to the back of the garden.

'Mum set this off the year we moved in.' A towering hawthorn displayed a mass of deep green leaves and white berries. Laura snipped a few mistletoe branches and dropped them into the basket she carried. 'Right… into the woods.'

They didn't have to walk far before they reached the woodlands behind the stone wall. There were a mix of trees, but pine trees were a plenty. They snipped off several appropriate branches and then walked further in to find some holly bushes.

After her father's warning, Laura wanted to build a bit of a barrier between herself and Carter. Having given it some thought on the walk so far, she stopped and turned to look at him.

'Can I ask you something?'

'Sure.' Carter shrugged, not too sure what was coming.

She'd meant to ask outright if Lizzie was his girlfriend, but she bottled it and changed her mind. 'You seem to have changed in the few days you've been here. Are you really going to go home when your holiday has finished and go back to living in seclusion?'

A shadow fell over Carter's face. He started walking again, and she took a few hurried steps to stay with him.

'I don't mean to pry, sorry. It's just I've come to care for you and the thought of you returning to your... quiet life, well I would wish more than that for you.' There, that gave him an opening to declare that actually he had a life with Lizzie.

'I've been thinking about Julie and Daniel a lot lately.'

She tilted her head, longing to ask who they were.

As if reading her thoughts he said, 'My adoptive parents. When I came out of hospital I went into the care system. I spent nine months in a home, and then Julie and Daniel became my kinship carers. They took me home and piled love on me. Eighteen months later, they asked if they could adopt me. I said yes, I mean why not. I think they thought I might mellow a bit towards them after that, but I didn't. I didn't want to let anyone in.' Carter stopped talking and walking. He just stood still staring at nothing.

'You didn't want to be hurt again.'

Carter slowly turned to look at her. She saw pain in his eyes. Every part of her wanted to pull him into a hug and hold him close. But she couldn't, he belonged to Lizzie. She couldn't break boundaries like that.

'In different ways both my father and mother hurt me. We're born to believe that our parents should love and care for us. It's a brutal betrayal when we find out they don't.'

Laura's response was automatic and flowed from her heart. 'We have one parent who will never hurt us. His love is unconditional and never ending.'

'I did pray once. He never responded.'

'He hears our every prayer, and although we may think He didn't reply, He did. One day we will see how, for today we live in trust.'

'Go on, say it.'

'What?'

'The Bible verse you're longing to say. I can feel it crackling in the air between us.'

'In the New Living Translation, John 3:16 tells us – For this is how God loved the world: He gave his one and only son, so that everyone who believes in Him will not perish but have eternal life.'

During her quote, Laura had taken two steps and now they stood face-to-face. Birds tweeted nearby. The wind rustled through the trees, shaking their branches and causing clumps of snow to fall with muted thuds.

'How did you know?' Laura asked. They stood so close that Carter could smell her minty breath.

The world rolled away from his consciousness, exaggerating the rise and fall of his chest. Each breath paused, then released with a keen sense of expectancy. 'I don't know. I could just feel it coming, I can't really explain how.'

'I believe God is trying to reach you.'

For the briefest moment, Carter's heart stopped beating. When it started again, it pounded his ribs like a caged man trying to escape.

'Where's this holly at?'

Clearly disappointed, Laura pointed ahead.

They set off, no more words between them, just the crunch of the freshly fallen snow beneath their feet.

EVERYONE ARRIVED IN GOOD TIME for the one and only rehearsal. Ted was in his element. Wearing bright blue flares and a flowered shirt, he carried his clipboard and barked orders getting everyone into position.

'Right then, order, order,' he called above the din of excited chatter. 'This is going to be the simplest nativity in history. You're basically going to walk forward when I tell you and then position yourself around the crib in the makeshift stable. I'm going to narrate the story and Sharon is going to read out various Bible scriptures. At certain points I'm going to press the CD player and we're going to sing along to some well-known tunes – yes, yes... I know Emily, not exactly hymns or carols, but groovy and fun and if you place Jesus in the centre of them, well they're just *right on!'*

Ted had to do a lot of shouting, but an hour and a half later he sighed happily, believing they all understood their parts.

'So that's a wrap folks. I'm sure the audience will dig it. I think we've done the best we can with such short time and hardly any cast.'

Laura grinned. 'You've done an amazing job, Ted. Totally groovy!'

'Hear, hear!' clapped Sharon.

'Any whippersnapper could have done it,' grumbled Joseph.

'You did a grand job too, Joseph.' Maeve wrapped her arm around his shoulder and kissed his cheek, and then stood straight again. 'Right then, we've measured the three crowns now. We just need to decorate them. I've got lots of star stickers and tubes of glitter. Do I have any volunteers to help me?'

Mykyta, Ivanna and Matthew all jumped up and cried out, 'Me!'

Joseph sat immobile, red coloured his cheekbones.

'Are you alright there, Joseph?' asked Laura.

'Darn it! The woman kissed me! What was she thinking? Has she gone off her rocker? Crazy old bat!'

Laura leaned close to his ear. 'Behave,' she warned him. 'We can always send you home you know.'

'But she…'

Laura raised one eyebrow and Joseph stopped talking.

'Grapes on a vine!' blurted out Carter.

'What?' Joseph scrunched up his face.

133

Laura shook her head at Carter and then explained to Joseph what he was trying to do.

'You'll have to do better than that!' snapped Joseph. 'Now, how about helping an old man into the lounge so I can sit next to the fire?'

Carter went over and offered the old grump his arm to lean on. The marvel that he didn't recoil each time he touched someone ran through him yet again. Maybe there was hope for him yet?

'That Maeve Appleby is reet forward, don't you think? I mean, the woman kissed me!'

'Unbelievable!'

''Tis, aye!'

'Yeah, that a sweet lady like Ms Appleby should want to kiss such a kind, distinguished young man like yourself, well that's just awful.'

Joseph growled, but stopped talking.

'Hey everyone,' called Sharon to the pub full of people. 'I think it might be a good idea if you head for home now. Look at the snow!'

Everyone rushed to the windows, except for Joseph who snuggled into his favourite chair and pulled a tartan blanket over his knees.

The snow flurry hid everything in white. Thick, white cotton wool style flakes seemed at once both gentle and slow and dangerous. People hurried to put on their coats, hats, scarves and gloves, and then rushed to their cars.

'Will they be alright?' asked Carter watching them go.

'They know the drill, slow and steady. Plus the snow is fresh and not frozen so they'll be OK.' Laura finally pulled herself away from the hypnotic snowfall. 'I can bring you some lunch into the quiet room, if that's where you're going to be writing? Is there anything on the menu you fancy today?'

'Would it be a bother to have some butternut squash soup?'

'Not at all, good choice by the way. I make it with ginger and crème fraîche, it's yummy if I say so myself.'

'I look forward to it.'

Snow, Snow, Snow

December 23, 2022

LIAM CALLAGHAN'S FRUSTATION GREW with each moment he argued with the police.

'But I live there. I've got to get home to my son.'

'I'm sorry, Sir. The road ahead is closed. The snow ploughs are out and about on the main roads but I'm afraid the road to Berrycombe probably won't be cleared any time soon.'

After a very frustrating fifteen minutes, and now soaked and cold from the falling snow, Liam finally got back in his car. He did a very slow three-point turn and headed back up the main road. What was he going to do? He drove a short distance and then pulled over to think.

Joanne didn't know he was on his way home. He'd wanted it to be a big surprise. He planned to smoother her with gifts and sweet words until she accepted him back with open arms, like she always did. He'd had it all planned and worked out in his mind. At first, when he'd got the posting on a North Sea oil rig he hadn't told her about it because he hadn't wanted her to know how much money he was earning.

Two weeks ago when the other crew members began talking about their excitement about returning to their families for Christmas, Liam had begun to experience regret and shame. All his life everything he touched had turned to rubbish. He was the biggest failure in history in his own mind. Joanne and Matthew were better off without him. He planned to send her some money to assuage his guilt. Yet something had happened to his determination to stay away from them. The homesickness he always felt each time he ran away, rose stronger and stronger the nearer to Christmas it got.

Joanne would have the tree up by now. Matthew would have sent a list to Father Christmas. Well, he hoped Matthew still believed. Liam had the magic of Christmas taken away from him at the age of four. His dad had told him there was no such thing as Father Christmas or Jesus for that matter. The declaration had come just moments before he'd packed his bags and left. Leaving Liam, his mother and three sisters alone and broke on Christmas Eve.

He'd never wanted to be like his dad, but the more he fought it, the more his dad's personality had materialised in him.

He glanced at the large pile of wrapped presents on the back seat and the threat of tears stung his eyes. He'd wanted to do something memorable for the pair of them. He loved them so much; he just struggled to be the person they expected him to be.

He thumped the steering wheel, but anger receded as bitter disappointment sank in. 'Stupid bobbin apples!' He whacked the wheel again but he couldn't stop the tears. He dropped his forehead onto the steering wheel and let them flow.

From somewhere he recalled his mother's sweet voice, 'Trust in the Lord with all your heart and lean not on your own understanding; in all your ways submit to him, and he will make your paths straight.' Proverbs 3:5-6 NIV

He'd believed when he was young, but the paths he'd chosen led to constant disappointment so he'd pushed the Lord out of his life. Maybe it was time to admit he couldn't make it on his own? He clasped his hands together and prayed for the first time in many years.

By the time he'd finished, he knew exactly what he was going to do.

CARTER PACED HIS ROOM. He'd wanted to ask Laura out for a meal, he'd thought maybe they could have driven to Kendal, but Bill had just informed him the roads were closed. He could kick himself. He wanted to buy Laura a present, Bill too. They'd looked after him so well since he'd arrived, they treated him like family. Now the shops were unreachable.

Just then he heard Mykyta and Ivanna laughing as they ran down the corridor chatting away ten to the dozen in Ukrainian. He heard the front door slam and got up to look out of the window. The children had gone out to make a snowman. It brought back a memory of building a snowman with Daniel. The man had done everything he could to bring Carter out of his shell, he could see that now. He reached for his mobile, maybe he should call them?

His hand dropped. *What would I say?* Maybe in the New Year he would pay them a visit, maybe. He opened the laptop. *Time to write!* He was enjoying this new story, it seemed lighter than his previous books.

Twenty minutes later, he pushed himself away from the table. He couldn't concentrate. All he wanted was to be with Laura. He paced a little, and then making up his mind went downstairs in search of Bill.

Bill, as per usual, was in the kitchen.

'Umm, what you baking now?'

Bill looked up as Carter came in and grinned. 'I have a honey-roast ham in the oven.'

'Smells heavenly.'

'Tastes even better, trust me!'

'I do.' Carter went over to the kitchen table and sat down.

'Would you like a coffee? I've made a filter pot over there, just help yourself.'

'Great, thanks.' Carter got up and fetched himself a cup of black coffee and then came back to the table where Bill sat hunched over a recipe book. 'I wouldn't have thought you still needed a cook book.'

'I don't for the things I cook over and over, but every now and again I like to have a read through for a bit of inspiration.'

'And have you been inspired today?'

'Yes, I'm looking mainly for the buffet tomorrow. I don't know how many people will come because of the snow, but I want to make sure I have enough in case we have a full house.

139

On the other hand I can't afford to waste any money so anything I make needs to be able to be frozen for another day if we don't eat it.'

'Ah, I can see that would limit your menu.'

'I'm going to make small sausage rolls, Cornish pasties and mini cheese and onion quiches. They can all be frozen if cooked from fresh. And of course, I'll be doing a hotpot, people will expect it.'

'Do you have everything you need? I mean shopping is out of the question I guess.'

Bill laughed. 'We're fully stocked, luckily. I did a huge shop at Costco last week and Mark dropped off all our vegetables this morning.'

'He ventured out in this?'

Bill chuckled again. 'We're used to the weather. He came on his tractor. So you've no need to worry, you won't be going hungry.'

'I wasn't worried, I was just curious.'

Bill's eyes twinkled at him, and Carter realized they were the exact same colour as Laura's, which brought him to the point.

'Bill I wanted to take Laura out for a meal today, but as the roads are closed that's now not an option.'

'Oh, aye.' Bill shuffled in his seat and sat up straight, his face suddenly unusually stern.

'That got me to thinking, and I wondered if you could cook us a special meal here? Obviously I will pay, I don't mean a freebie. Do you think she would accept a date with me?'

'Carter, I've come to like you well enough. But I'll not have you playing around with my daughter's affection. If the roads were open, I'd ask you to leave so I would!'

'Celery batons! Bill, I wouldn't mess Laura about.'

'Eh?'

'Celery doesn't work?'

Bill shook his head.

Carter tried again to convince Bill. 'I really like Laura, I mean a lot. I want nothing more than the chance to get to know her some more.'

'What about Lizzie?'

'Lizzie?'

'Yes, how can you say you want to date my daughter when you already have a woman in your life?'

'Ha,' Carter sat back in his chair and grinned at Bill. 'I don't know how you know about Lizzie, but she's my motherly PA, she's a happily married grandmother. Quite honestly I'd be lost without her, but she's not *mine*.'

'Ah, I see. Well that changes everything. What would you like to eat?'

Carter grinned and leaned forward again. 'What's Laura's favourite meal?'

'You son, are my kind of man!'

With the menu planned out, Carter went in search of Laura. He found her putting the final pieces of the hearth wreath together. Just pine boughs with holly and mistletoe woven through, and tiny red bows throughout.

'It looks grand.'

Laura turned around and grinned at him. 'Thank you.'

'Laura?'

'Yes?'

'I wondered if you would have dinner with me tonight? Just the two of us in the breakfast room.'

Her smile dropped, and after his conversation with Bill he knew why.

'Lizzie is my PA not my girlfriend. Later, when she's awake we can give New York a call and you can have a chat with her if you like? She's dying to say hello to you!'

'She is?'

'Actually, she is. Will you have dinner with me after the choir practice that is? That's if anyone can make it with all this snow.'

Pink flushed Laura's cheeks, she gave a shy smile. 'Yes, thank you, I would like to have dinner with you.'

'Great! I've sorted the menu with your dad; he said to tell you that you've officially been given the night off.'

'Well that would be grand if he paid me!'

'Oh, darn cherry tomatoes!' Carter swung his right arm in front of him and clicked his fingers.

Laura pursed her lips and slowly shook her head.

'Keep trying?'

She nodded several times.

'Right, gotta go. See you at seven for singing practice.'

Laura's eyes were sparkling. 'See you then.' She watched Carter rush from the room, her heartbeat racing. He was single after all! How blooming *carrot tops* good was that?

Now, the path to the main road needed clearing. She collected helpers and shovels and they set off to clear a walkway through the two-feet high snowfall.

LIAM PACED SHAUN'S FLOOR. 'Trust me I know what I'm doing, I can make it.'

Shaun shook his head. 'You're mad. Just call her and tell her you got stuck here. She'll understand. She wouldn't want you risking your life to get home for Christmas.'

'You don't understand. They don't know I'm coming, it's a surprise. I've got to do this. Please help me out, Shaun.'

'Have you ever even walked in snowshoes before?'

'When we were kids. Come on, how hard can it be? You can drive me along the Underbarrow Road, that's still open, although I hear it might be closing any moment now. If you can drop me off near Grigghall, I'll be able to cut across the moors from there. I know the way in my sleep. I'll be fine.'

'I think it's a terrible plan, Liam.'

'Mate,' Liam put his hands together in a pleading way.

'Is your phone fully charged? The signal's not always great around there but you should be able to call emergency services if you get stuck.'

'I won't need to, honest. I'll be fine. Will you lend me your snowshoes and can you drop me off?'

Shaun shook his head but said, 'OK, but you can't go now, it'll be dark soon. We'll go in the morning when it's light. And if the main road's also closed then you can forget it. Deal?'

'Deal, thanks bud.'

CARTER HAD ENCOURAGED EMILY to come and stand close to the piano. Not that he wanted to drown her out, although effectively that's what he did, earning the thanks of all the other eleven singers. He figured yesterday that her hearing wasn't great, by placing her close to the piano she could hear the melody clearly and somehow that kept her more in tune.

They had chosen five carols to sing the next day and they went through each of them twice. Carter marvelled that they'd all turned up.

'City boy!' Joseph called him. 'You never heard of good boots and warm clothes? I'm telling ya, there's no such thing as bad weather, only badly dressed people.'

Bill turned up at the end of the session with a warm glass of mulled wine for the adults and hot chocolate for the children, to warm them ready for the cold walk home.

'Saint you are, Bill my mate,' said Joseph helping himself to a glass from the tray.

'Hey, you don't have to walk home,' laughed Bill.

'Yes, but all that singing has given me a right thirst, wouldn't begrudge an old man would 'ee?'

'Bah! Singing? You did nought more than grumble through that whole lot Joseph Tanner, so you did.'

'No one asked your opinion Maeve Appleby! If we didn't have Laura, Sue and Elmer singing, the rest of you'd be snowballed out of town!'

'Joseph! Would you want me to be a-kissing you again! No? I didn't think so. Best be quiet is what I'm thinking!' Maeve burst out laughing. 'Silly old man! Got to love you though.'

'I'm sure you don't!' Joseph squealed.

CARTER CHECKED HIS APPEARANCE in the mirror. He couldn't put his suit on, it would be too formal, but he wanted to look nice. He splashed on a little cologne. He wore black trousers and a black polo neck jumper. He hoped Laura would like it. The darkness of the clothes made his grey eyes appear lighter. He peered forward. *Where has the old me gone?*

He straightened up again. It was time to go. He couldn't believe how nervous he felt. *Is Laura feeling the same way?*

He reached the breakfast room first. Bill had set up a table in front of the log fire, which burned brightly for the first time since he'd arrived. Music came from speakers on the wall. As planned, Bill had put on what he called his 'peaceful playlist.' Right now, Enya filled the room at just the right volume.

He looked at the table with appreciation. Bill had set up a white table cloth, flowers and candles, you couldn't get more romantic.

Just then the door opened, and Carter looked up.

Laura took his breath away. Gone were the comfy jeans and jumpers she'd been wearing lately. In their place a simple mauve dress completely flattered her slight figure and pretty face. Her hair for once hung loose and the soft brown tresses bounced on her shoulders.

For a moment they got lost in each other's eyes, and then Carter remembered his manners. He pulled back a chair, 'Madam.'

She came and sat down. Carter shook out a folded napkin and offered it to her.

She chuckled and accepted it. 'Why thank you sir.'

He picked up a bottle of red wine and held it so she could see the label. 'To your liking?'

'Very much.'

He took the corkscrew, and opened the wine pouring them both a glass before sitting down. He raised his glass. 'Good health.'

Laura took hers and clinked it against his. 'Cheers.'

With great timing Sharon came into the room carrying two plates of spaghetti carbonara, her grin *very* wide. She put the plates on the table, 'Bon appétit!'

'Thank you,' both Carter and Laura said at the same time.

They talked a little over the food, but real conversation only started when they'd finished. She told him all about Ethan, and how he'd left just before Christmas piling more unhappiness onto memories of the season. He pumped her with questions and she talked for a long time about her mum and how her dad had fallen apart when she'd died.

'I'm sorry for all your sadness. If I could take it away I would.'

'That's kind of you, Carter, but there is no life that doesn't have to go through suffering. Without it we would have no understanding of good times or blessed moments. And I know I will meet my mother again in Heaven, it's a joy that I look forward to.'

'It must be nice to have such faith.'

'I can't imagine a life without it. God is my rock and my strength. I don't think I could cope without Him.'

'Julie and Daniel tried their best to teach me about God, but the walls I'd built around myself were just too hard for them to get through. I'd shut my mind down against anything to do with love, I just didn't want to know.'

'Do you remember much about your birth mum?'

'Unfortunately, yes. Though from sessions with my counsellor I now doubt exactly how many of them are true. I didn't understand that the brain can manipulate events and make you remember in an incorrect way.'

'I didn't know that.'

'It's a thing apparently. I do remember waking up in hospital on Christmas Day, a pile of concerned faces around the bed. One nurse couldn't stop crying. They didn't let me look in the mirror for a week, but even when I did look after all that time, my face was still swollen and black. That's a true memory. It's been tormenting me ever since it happened.'

Laura gasped.

'Please don't feel sorry me. That's not why I'm talking to you about it.'

It was hard to talk because of the lump in her throat. 'It's almost impossible not to. You'd be upset for any child who went through that.'

'True. But I'm not a child anymore, I grew up.'

'Thank the Lord, you're still here.'

'Back then, the bruises caused by my mother, both physical and mental, were clear for everyone to see. A cocaine user doesn't know what they're doing, that's what I've always told myself. It wasn't personal that she didn't love or care for me. I was an activity-by-product that she wanted no part of; those were the last words from her I ever heard. But all these years later, I still suffer from the fear of rejection.'

'That's understandable.'

'You don't think less of me because I'm in therapy?'

'Not at all. Only brave people face their problems.'

They carried on talking for another half-an-hour and then Laura declared she needed her sleep ready for the big day tomorrow.

'Do you think the bad weather will put people off coming tomorrow?'

'We're a hardy bunch around here. People will come if they can.'

They stood at the same time. Without thinking they moved close to one another. Carter searched her eyes for permission to kiss her. He thought he saw it and moved towards her lips.

'Hey, you two! Are you ready to call it a night?' Bill came in larger than life, and the two of them pulled away from each other.

'Yes, Dad. We were just about to turn in, tomorrow is a big day!'

Pylons Down

Christmas Eve, 2022

CHRISTMAS EVE DID NOT START the way everyone would have liked. A fierce, unprecedented, storm and blizzard had hit Cumbria during the night, and when Berrycombe woke it was to a cold dark morning... with no electricity. To make matters worse, the telephones were also down.

Yet small towns have their own little ways, and before long everyone knew they were welcome to spend the day at the Berry Inn to keep warm. The pub not only had an Aga and several log and coal fires, but the emergency generator would mean they would have electricity for a few hours at least. Hopefully, by the time it ran out of petrol, the mains electricity would be back on. A tour was completed by tractor until everyone was content that not a person had been left out of the invitation. Not long after seven o'clock in the morning, people started arriving. A few of the villagers had huge Land Rovers with tyres made for the bad weather and they went around collecting people who either had no transport or cars that would simply slip and slide over the roads.

They flooded in, a bustle of loud activity. Laura began to fret about how they would cater for so many. She needn't have worried. Between them they yielded a mass of goodies from their homes and piled into the kitchen to offer up their food and help.

So many people crammed into his domain that Bill eventually had to shoo most of them away. By nine o'clock most people had eaten breakfast and settled into the main lounge, where the fire blazed. Soon the board games and cards were out.

SHAUN TOOK A LOT of persuading but eventually he drove Liam through the heavy snowfall as far as he could.

'I think you're crazy man. You should stay with me until they clear the roads.'

'Thanks Shaun, but I've gotta get home.'

'You're going to look like Father Christmas with that red sack!'

'Ha! I am a bit! And hey, red is good. If I get lost in the snow you'll be able to spot the red bag a mile off.'

'Whatever you do, don't get lost!'

'I'll try not to.'

They came together for a brief hug and a lot of back slapping. 'Take care, and whatever you do, don't stop. Just keep going until you get there, even if you feel like you're dying.'

'Thanks Shaun. I promise I'll take care.'

Shaun stood by the side of the road. He watched his old school mate traipse across the field that led to the moors, the red sack bouncing on his back. A part of him felt sick that his friend was taking such a risk, another part admired him.

EMILY SAT IN THE CORNER away from the others, her knitting needles clicking away ten to the dozen. She'd ordered herself a sherry, (for the warmth) and surrounded herself with piles of wool. She'd started a jumper for her granddaughter who lived in Australia. It was thick and fluffy and probably much more suited to the cold weather of Cumbria.

'You knitting me a jumper?' asked Joseph, who sat comfortably in the chair next to her, a book on his lap.

'It's for my Samantha.'

'I thought she lived in Mildura?'

'She does.'

'But isn't it like… hot all year round there?'

'To us it might be, but June is their winter and even though we'd find it warm I'm sure they feel the cold.'

'Cold enough to wear a thick woolly jumper?'

'I think so.'

'Isn't that a Christmas tree on the pattern?'

'It is. I thought she'd like something English to wear on Christmas Day next year.'

'I'm confused; you just said their winter…'

'Cherry pips! I know what I said, old man!'

Joseph shuffled in his seat and when he was comfortable he opened the book on his lap. Under his breath he moaned, 'Rhubarb sticks! Give me Maeve any day!'

'Did you call?'

Joseph startled and looked up to find Maeve hovering over his seat. 'No! Indeed I didn't!' He flicked through the pages as if looking for his place. 'Now where was I?'

'I'm sure I heard you call me.'

Joseph ignored her and pretended to read.

She ruffled his thin grey hair. 'You are a grump, but I do love you.'

Joseph coughed until he sounded like he was choking.

'Goodness me, let me fetch you a glass of water.' Maeve rushed away.

Emily laughed. 'Why don't you just marry the woman?'

When his coughing gave up at last, he sighed and reclined in the seat again. 'We're too old for all that shenanigans.'

'No one is too old for love!' Maeve pushed a glass of water at him and when he took it she went storming off.

'She's loved you since she was sixteen.'

'Yes, but I married Daisy and I swear I never gave Maeve any encouragement.'

'As you say, but Daisy has been gone a *very* long time now Joseph. Why don't you have a bit of companionship in your last days?'

'Laura! Laura!'

Laura turned around to see Mykyta and Ivanna charging across the room towards her.

'Whoa, whoa, slow down. There are too many people in here, you'll cause an accident.'

Ivanna blurted out a long sentence in excited Ukrainian.

Laura bent down and put her hands on her knees. Before she could ask what she'd said, Mykyta told her in English.

'Papa sent a text. He's zapping us!'

'Zapping?' said Laura.

Anna came rushing over laughing. 'Pavlo speak. He zooming to watch children.'

Laura straightened up. 'Oh, that's lovely news. Did you tell him we were hoping to do the nativity at three o'clock today?'

'Tak, yes. He said should be no problem.'

'Marvellous! We'll have to make sure everyone is ready at the right time. How fab!'

'Best gift,' said Anna.

Laura wrapped her arm around the beaming woman. 'It is indeed.'

'I wish my dad could see me be a shepherd,' said Matthew looking mighty glum.

Carter appeared behind him. He put his hand on Matthew's shoulder. 'I bet your dad wished for nothing more than to be with you. I'm sure he would be here if he could.'

Matthew shrugged out of Carter's touch. 'I've prayed for a miracle. I hear God does them sometimes. But... I don't think my dad loves me anymore.'

'I'm sure he does,' said Laura. She looked at his face and just wanted to wrap him in her arms. 'Right, I'm about to start baking shortbread and gingerbread biscuits. Does anyone want to help?'

Besides the three children, Martha and Hyacinth both overheard and offered to come and help. Carter happily followed them into the kitchen. He'd never made cookies in his life but it sounded fun.

Laura glanced over her shoulder at him as they walked. 'Have you seen Ted?'

He shook his head.

An hour and a half later the pub smelled of biscuits, but Ted still hadn't showed up.

'Dad, do you know if anyone reached Ted this morning?'

Ted's house was the furthest away out of the village, but only by about an extra twenty-minute walk.

'I think Tucker mentioned that he'd seen him and told him he was welcome at the pub all day. He's got his own Aga though, so his house will be warm. He's probably waiting until nearer the time of the show before he comes.'

'Children, why don't you take a plate of biscuits each and offer them to everyone in the lounge?'

They happily accepted their task and went off full of pride over their homemade goodies.

'Right Dad, let us help you with the hotpot and vegetable soup. What do you need us to do?'

Carter grinned, Laura had automatically included him. He felt like part of the family.

'All the pies are made. Carter, how are you with a peeler? We need that mountain of vegetables peeling.'

'Jumping junipers! I'm on it, boss!' He squared his shoulders and grinned.

Laura and Bill groaned.

'Still not there?'

They shook their heads.

'Will you make the soup, love?'

'Sure.'

Bill turned on jolly Christmas tunes and it was impossible not to sing along as they worked. Rocking around the Christmas tree was sung with such gusto that several people came in to see what was going on.

Everything was going according to plan. In an hour the nativity would start, shortly followed by a carol service.

A bang sounded through the kitchen, the lights flickered and then went out. Although it was only two o'clock with the heavy cloud cover it went as dark as night. Bill had prepared lamps in advance of losing the generator. The first one flicked to life within moments.

Sharon came rushing in from the bar.

'Here you are.' Bill passed her the first lamp and then lit the next. Shortly the kitchen, lounge and hallway were lit with a slow, yellow flickering light from paraffin lamps.

Carter came and stood close to Laura, without hesitating she slipped her hand into his. Warmth surged through his chest.

Make Haste for the Inn

Christmas Eve, 2022

LIAM'S NOSE HAD GONE from stinging cold to numb. Not a good sign. The bag on his back had been getting heavier and heavier with each passing moment. His steps, at first fast and light, had become slow and heavy. His chest pained him terribly and he finally understood his folly. This wasn't the weather to be out and about in. He should have stayed at Shaun's. What on earth had he been thinking?

He stopped for a moment, his chest heaving. He wanted nothing more than to sit down and give himself a rest. He pulled off a glove and shoved his hand in his pocket. He'd call Joanne; let her know he was trying to get home.

He swiped it on. 'Oh no!' The absence of bars showed the lack of a signal. He'd known it might happen. The signal was always hit-and-miss around here. He put the phone away and shoved his hand quickly back into the glove. There was nothing for it but to keep going forward.

He had a sneaky feeling he should have arrived in Berrycombe by now, but he couldn't even see any lights from the village. He didn't want to admit he was lost, but dread was building and filling his stomach with acid.

TED WAS CROSS WITH himself for leaving it so late to go to the pub. He'd woken with a headache and although he'd been up when Tucker had knocked on his door, shortly after that he'd thought to take ten minutes on the sofa. Only he'd slept most of the day.

'They're going to be stressing. Not good, not good.' He checked the time again. Two o'clock. He had enough time to grab a sandwich before he went. As he buttered his bread, he gazed out of the kitchen window. Snow was falling heavily.

TAKING A WELL-EARNED BREAK from the cooking and washing up, Carter sat down on the floor near the fireplace and rested his back against the wall. He'd thought about going upstairs for a little privacy, but in the end decided it was too cold.

'You alright there, son?' asked Joseph.

'Sure, just taking five.'

'I've been watching you.'

'You have?'

'Yes. I think you should stay. You fit in.'

'My home's in New York. I can't imagine living anywhere else.'

Joseph kept his gaze on the page of the book he wasn't reading. 'I shouldn't imagine Laura could imagine living anywhere but here in Berrycombe.'

'You never know.'

'I know she gave up a promising singing career to stay with t'ol fella, I canna see her jetting off across the world without him.'

'We don't even know how we feel about each other yet. I think making plans for the future would be a bit presumptuous of me.'

'We only live once, son. Don't get to your deathbed and wish things had been different. Do something about it now.' Joseph picked up his book and pretended to read. He'd not been able to read a thing since his glasses broke last year, but he'd be darned if he would let this lot know.

FROZEN TEARS STUNG LIAM'S cheeks. He was such an idiot. He'd lost all feeling in his feet and hands. All he wanted to do was lie down and go to sleep. The snow reflected white back up into the sky, yet still his vision hazed and blurred as if he walked through volcanic ash. He finally admitted to himself that he had no clue where he was.

He longed to drop the red elephant on his back onto the snow. The gifts he'd imagined bringing joy now resembled nothing more than back-breaking burdens. Sheer determination prevented him from letting the red sack slip to the ground. He knew once it did, he'd never pick it up again.

On he trudged. One step after another. That's all he could see. He'd stopped looking up and ahead of him ages ago. Now he watched as each foot came into view and then disappeared again. One foot, then the other. Didn't every long journey begin with a single step? He wanted this journey over.

'Sorry, Joanne. I'm so sorry.' Another tear fell and froze as it slid down his ice-chilled skin.

TED TURNED THE KEY to start his old Range Rover. Clunk – clunk. 'Oh come on! Give me a break!'

He tried again… and again. It refused to start. He sat in his seat looking out of the windscreen. He'd just taken fifteen minutes to clear all the snow off the car and to de-ice the frozen lock. Now it wouldn't even start!

He sighed and a stream of steam flew from his nostrils. He didn't own a mobile phone and the landline was down. He couldn't call anyone for a lift. He could walk but it was at least thirty maybe forty minutes in this weather. He'd be too late for the show. Plus, although he was fairly sprightly he didn't trust his legs in this blizzard.

He got out of the car and went back inside the cottage. He'd try the phone again, maybe a miracle would have happened and BT might have fixed it already.

'HE'S GOT THE SCRIPT, how can we do the nativity without him? I've got to go and check he's OK, Dad. I've just got to. I know he would be here if everything was fine.'

'It's too dangerous to drive out there. I'm sure he's OK. He's probably having car trouble. You know how old his car is, it breaks down all the time.'

'We could go in mine,' offered Carter.

'That's kind of you, but I don't think even yours could handle the snow and ice on the roads right now. We haven't seen a gritter for three days, everything will be covered.'

Laura gnawed on her knuckles. Carter didn't know what to do to help her.

Bill raised a hand with a pointed finger. 'We could walk to Tanner Farm. I'm sure Alfred will lend us his tractor again, but it's mighty freezing out there.'

'I'll go,' said Carter immediately.

'And I'm going with you. You won't know the way to Ted's place.'

'I'll get the large torch for you; you're going to need it.' Bill went off to the store room, swinging a lamp as he went.

'You're going to be glad of your arctic gear now,' said Laura with a grin. 'Put on as many layers as you can. It's layers that hold the warmth. Meet you by the front door in ten.'

'I'll be there.'

Ten minutes later, they set off armed with the industrial-sized torch. With scarves wrapped around their faces, only their eyes were visible, meaning trying to talk was pointless. Laura led the way and Carter stayed as close to her as he could. She stumbled a few times, each time Carter swooped in and caught her before she hit the snow-covered ground.

Alfred's farmhouse had a welcoming orange glow flooding from the downstairs windows. After a few hefty knocks, he opened the door.

'Come on in,' he cried, helping to pull them in so he could close the door as quickly as possible.

'What in Heaven's name brings you out in a storm like this?'

'We need to check on Ted. I've come to ask if we could borrow the tractor again, Alfred.'

'For sure you can. It's in the barn. Hold on, let me just wrap up and we'll fetch it out.'

'Thank you. We'll bring it straight back of course.'

'No need, I was coming to the Berry shortly anyway. I'll walk over and drive the tractor home later.'

'Ah, that's great, cheers.'

They made a dash to the barn and Alfred opened the doors wide. 'You good to drive it out, Laura lass? I'll shut doors after you.'

'Yes, no problem.'

Laura and Carter climbed the gigantic steps up the tractor.

'You got a full pub?'

'Yes, most of the people still in the village have come over to keep warm.'

'Is t'ol fella feeding them all?'

Laura laughed. 'Any excuse to entertain and play host, you know Dad. He's made a hotpot and tons of pastries, so don't have any tea before you come over whatever you do. We *literally* have enough to feed a small army!'

'Steve, from over tha' way, popped in earlier. You know he uses a walkie-talkie to keep in touch with his brother over in Richmond?'

'Yeah.'

'Well Seth told Steve that it's been on the news that they don't think they'll be able to fix the power lines for another twenty-four hours, so looks like we'll not have electricity tomorrow either. Guess you'll be hosting everyone tomorrow as well?'

'Looks like it then.'

'Well hold on just one moment, I've got something you can have.' He rushed back to the farmhouse and came out shortly with a huge bag which he put in the back behind their seats.

'What's that?'

'A turkey and a pile of sausages, and hold on, I've got some wood for you too.' He ran off down the side of the barn and came back with his arms filled with wood. 'You tell t'ol fella that if he's running low he's just to come back and get some more.'

'You're very kind Alfred, thank you very much. I'm sure everyone will appreciate it.'

'You'll be going past Steve's, call in there too. He mentioned he has some coal and wood you could have.'

'Thanks, will do.'

The lights of the tractor flooded the path before them. A white splash of beauty reflected back at them and took their breath away.

'It's beautiful isn't it,' said Carter once they were on their way.

'Beautiful, but deadly.'

IT TURNS OUT CRYING ISN'T such a good idea when you're freezing. His eyelashes had stuck, closing one eye completely. Liam peered through one eye and surveyed the land in front of him. No village in sight. No lights indicating farms either, very odd. The land around was littered with farms, he should have come across one by now.

It dawned on him slowly that he might have walked in a circle. 'If I've done that Lord, you're really going to have to help me, for without a miracle I'm going to die out here.'

He took his phone out of his pocket again and looked for a signal bar. It took ages as his fingers refused to work properly. None. He tilted his head backward and screamed his frustration at the sky.

The sack of presents slid off his back and landed in the snow with a squelch and gentle thud.

AS SOON AS LAURA pulled the tractor into Ted's driveway, she could see him in the kitchen window. She waved. Even from this distance she could see the relief on his face. He waved back like crazy.

'Someone's pleased to see us,' laughed Carter.

They jumped down and hurried into the cottage. After Ted had opened the door for them, they stamped their boots on the doorstep and entered the hallway.

'Turn around,' he cried. 'We've got to get going.'

'It's OK Ted, don't panic. Everything for the nativity is in place. Everyone's ready too. We just need to get back that's all.'

'No. No. No. We're going across the moors first.'

'What? Why?' Laura turned to give Carter a worried frown. 'Are you OK, Ted?'

'I've still got all my marbles if that's what you're inferring. Now out! Quick! We've no time to lose.'

'Ted, what's the matter? Why do you want to go across the moors in weather like this?'

'Laura, we've got no time to lose! Let's go!'

Ted didn't bother locking the door after he pulled it shut. Carter walked to the side of him in case he should slip, and then he helped Ted climb the gigantic steps.

'Ted, I'm sorry but we need to get back to the pub,' said Laura turning on the ignition. The engine immediately bounced into life. She put it in gear and turned the tractor around in the drive with painstaking care.

'I heard a scream. Someone's on the moors.'

'Are you sure? It might have been an owl.'

Ted shook his head. 'I know the difference. We need to take a look.'

Laura looked over the top of Ted's head at Carter, he gave a short nod.

They couldn't risk going straight back to the pub if someone really was in trouble, so instead of turning right out of Ted's drive, Laura turned left.

BILL KEPT HIMSELF BUSY, but that didn't stop him from feeling sick. With each passing minute for the last fifteen minutes he'd been expecting Laura to return.

'I'll make us a cup of tea,' said Sharon.

Anna came into the kitchen in a fluster. 'Do you think we do play at four? Pavlo not good, some problem for calling. Laura agree?'

Sharon answered. 'I'm sure that will fit in just fine. Won't it Bill?'

Bill nodded.

Anna's shoulders dropped as she sighed. 'That is good, no. Thank you.'

After Anna had gone, Sharon and Bill sat down at the table.

'She should have been back by now.'

Sharon reached over and covered Bill's hand with hers. He turned to meet her warm eyes smiling at him. 'She'll be fine.'

For the first time since they'd known each other, Bill reached over and touched her face. 'You're my rock, Sharon, you know that right?'

'I've known it longer than you.'

'Thank you for being so patient.'

Sharon pulled away from the table and Bill's hand. 'Right! Let's go and tell everyone everything will be delayed an hour. I need to relieve Nick who's helping out behind the bar. He's been on his own for an hour now, poor lad.'

THEY HAD DRIVEN A LITTLE way down the lane and then pulled along the pathway that led across the moorland stretch. The tractor's headlights lit up everything like a lighthouse.

'If there is anyone out here, they'll surely see us coming,' said Carter. 'But I've got to be honest; I don't know how we're going to find anyone, especially if they've fallen down.'

'Laura girl, keep your eyes open, but pray will you?'

'I have been praying already, Ted. If anyone's really out here, if we don't find them, they're a gonner.'

'Power in unity, lass. Pray aloud.'

She didn't hesitate. 'Dear Father in Heaven, please hear our prayer. We thank you for Alfred's tractor and for its light. We thank you for the pub and the Aga and the log fires. We thank you that no one has been hurt during the storm. Thank you for this very special time of year when we remember the birth of your son. Oh Lord, I could thank You for so much, but please right now, I ask… if there is someone out here, please direct us to them. Amen.'

Both Ted *and* Carter said, 'Amen.' It warmed Laura's heart.

They pushed forward, leaving a path of crushed snow behind them. Two minutes went by, then three, then four. Laura concentrated on a safe place to drive while Ted and Carter swung their heads from left to right as if they were watching a tennis match, searching for a possible storm-casualty.

With the passing of each minute their hope began to fade.

'Maybe it was an owl,' said Ted at last.

'I think we should go back,' said Carter.

Laura, hunched over the wheel, peered ahead. 'Just two more minutes and then we'll swing back.'

They didn't find anyone.

Laura took particular care and drove the tractor in a small circle to return to the road. They were halfway back to the lane, when Carter jumped out of his seat.

'Over there,' he pointed.

'How did we miss him?' said Ted.

Laura kept driving until they were a few yards away. 'I'll keep the engine running.'

Carter jumped down in one go and raced to the body of a man sitting upright but covered in snow. He skidded to a halt beside him and started knocking the snow off the man's body. 'Oh, please still be alive!'

'Let me help.' Laura crouched on the other side of the man and began to rub his face with her bare hands. 'Oh my! It's Liam! What is he doing on the moors? Liam? Liam?'

His right lashes fluttered a few times and he looked at her. 'Where you been?' he whispered.

'Oh thank God,' said Laura. 'Come on, let's get you home.'

It took all their strength to help him up, and even more to get him up on the tractor. Eventually, they had him lying on the floor behind the seats.

'Carter, will you hold him and try to warm him? I'll get us back as quickly as I can.'

Carter slipped behind Liam and pulled him up so that Liam's back was against his chest. He wrapped his arms around him and tried willing his body warmth into the stranger.

At one stage, Liam's head dropped forward. Ted poked him. 'Come on son, stay awake.'

Liam lifted his head and laid it back against Carter's chest. 'Take me home, Laura. I need to see Jo and Matthew.'

Laura half turned her head. 'They're at the pub.'

BILL HAD BEEN WATCHING from his bedroom window that looked out over the car park. As soon as he saw the lights he flung his coat on and went charging down the stairs.

'We're OK, Dad, but we've found poor Liam. He's frozen through. He needs a warm drink and a warm bath as soon as possible.'

'Where's Jo?'

Bill took over from Laura and helped Carter support Liam under his arms.

'Let's get you warmed up first, shall we,' said Bill. 'You wouldn't want young Matthew seeing you like this, now would you?'

Liam shook his head.

'We'll go to my room,' said Bill.

Laura stood with Sharon at the bottom of the stairs watching the men go up.

'He was lucky. If we hadn't found him he'd have been dead by morning.'

Sharon wrapped an arm around Laura's shoulder. 'Thank God you found him. Now come into the kitchen, let's get some hot chocolate on the go.'

Laura took off her coat and boots and followed Sharon into the kitchen. 'The nativity is going to be ruined, isn't it? People will be wanting their supper soon, so they can go home.'

Sharon turned around from the kitchen unit and smiled at Laura. 'Pavlo can't get a connection until four. Everyone knows and they're ready. The pub is packed Laura, and trust me – no one is in a hurry to go home. Nothing is going to stop this from happening. Not a storm or a power cut. Everything will be perfect, just you wait and see.'

Candlelight Nativity

Christmas Eve, 2022

BY THE TIME THE CAT wailed for the third time, everyone began to tut. The previous silence (that had descended over the last hour) began to vanish as people shuffled in their chairs and rustled newspapers and things in an irritable way. The lack of power meant no television to watch and no music to listen to. The games, which had started out jolly, had now dwindled. The extra hour of waiting for the nativity felt like an eternity.

Meow!

'Oh, for crying out loud! Will someone let the blooming cat in before my eardrums burst?' grumbled Joseph.

'As it happens, I do,' replied Maeve, passing Joseph a packet of sweets.

'What?' Joseph's frown creased his whole face.

'Pear drops, drumsticks and Starburst, funny how you should ask for exactly the sweet mix that I have. You been spying on me again old man?' Her high-pitched tone didn't quite match the sly smile and fluttering eyelashes.

Brian stood, planning to let the cat in, but Ivanna appeared in the room cuddling a Siamese cat.

'That creature looks like a rat on steroids,' hissed Joseph.

Martha rapped her knitting needles against the table. 'And you look like a Staffordshire chewing a wasp! You grumpy drawers, you!'

Impossible though it seemed, Joseph's ruddy face went even redder. His bulbous, bumpy nose twitched in irritation. He ran a hand through his thin hair and snapped. 'You old sour puss!'

'Whose cat is it anyway?' Brian asked Emily.

Hyacinth raised her hand. 'She's wild. We think one of the summer rental families left her behind two years ago. She wanders the village looking for adoring fans more than food! She's mostly playful, when she's not whining that is.'

Ivanna approached Hyacinth. 'You want?'

Hyacinth shook her head. 'You cuddle her sweetheart, she loves lots of attention.'

Just then, Ted appeared. 'Ta-da! I'm here at last. Did you miss me?'

The happy greeting he'd been expecting wasn't forthcoming.

'Cheer up folk!' Ted tugged at the silk scarf tied around his neck and straightened his tinsel-covered halo. He was an interesting sight in his bright green shirt and red flares, topped off with a black leather waistcoat. But it was probably the big gold loop in his left ear that set him apart from the other pensioners.

Just then Laura appeared in the main doorway. She waved at Ted.

Ted picked up his clipboard. 'Thank goodness. Right everyone, positions please. We're about to begin.'

An excited hush descended.

Ivanna plopped the cat into Emily's lap and rushed out to join the others in the hallway. Her floor-length, blue-dyed, sheet-cut-into-a-toga rustled as she ran.

A small area beside the tree had been set up with the stable props from the church. Although the tree fairy lights weren't on, a few of the women raced around the many window sills lighting tealights and candles. The fire flickered and crackled and gas lamps sat on a few of the tables.

Ted took his position near the back of the room beside the bar. Without electricity the microphone didn't work, so he called out in his loudest voice. 'Ladies and gentlemen, family and friends, new and old, I welcome you to the Berry Inn Nativity. Sharon…'

Sharon opened her Bible and began to read…

'So Joseph also went up from the town of Nazareth in Galilee to Judea, to Bethlehem the town of David, because he belonged to the house and line of David. He went there to register with Mary, who was pledged to be married to him and was expecting a child. While they were there, the time came for the baby to be born, and she gave birth to her firstborn, a son. She wrapped him in cloths and placed him in a manger, because there was no guest room available for them.' Luke 2: 4-7 NIV

Ted pressed play on his battery-operated CD player. As the first chords started, Ted called out in his theatrical voice, 'Joseph and Mary would accept a stable as a shelter.' He paused a moment and waved at the children hovering outside in the hallway.

As Mykyta and Ivanna appeared in the door, dressed as Mary and Joseph, there was a general murmur through the crowd.

Ted continued. 'Imagine Jesus is singing to you.' He turned up the volume.

'Sometimes in our life we all have pain, we all have sorrow, but if we are wise, we know there is always tomorrow. Lean on me when you're not strong and I'll be your friend, I'll help you carry on.' Bill Withers: Lean on Me 1972

Mykyta pretended to help Ivanna walk to the stable by holding her arm, although he seemed more to be hindering her.

Laura heard Joseph mutter something about tradition, while Emily responded with something about new-fangled rubbish. 'Oh dear,' Laura whispered to herself.

Mykyta looked back at her and stopped walking across the room. She shoo'd him on with a smile and a wave of her hands. He looked to Anna. She sadly shook her head and shrugged.

'Oh Lord, if You could please connect Pavlo for the children, that would be just super.'

'Amen to that,' Bill whispered in her ear.

Laura looked up. 'Is he alright?'

'Yes. He's soaking in a warm bath, he'll be done soon.'

Ivanna sat down on the blanket by the makeshift dwelling, a wooden prop that if touched wobbled horrendously. Mykyta knelt beside her and wiped her brow with a large white cloth. Although part of the act, she knocked his hand away, making some people giggle.

Laura watched everyone anxiously; they didn't seem sure how to respond. She decided to sing. 'I'll help you carr'eee on.' She swayed from foot to foot and began to clap. Within moments the whole pub joined in with her, clapping in time and singing. Her joy skyrocketed! 'Lean on me when you're not strong and I'll be your friend, I'll help you carry on.'

Ted grinned at her and gave her the thumbs up.

At the end of the song, Ted lowered the volume and pressed pause. He gave a nod to Ivanna. She pulled a doll out from under the blanket, rocked it in her arms and then laid it on the straw in the crib.

Ted fought back a cough and took a deep breath to propel his voice out as loudly as he could. 'With the arrival of the child, Mary and Joseph gave thanks to God, for their baby had all his fingers and toes. Yet, I can imagine they weren't warm or comfortable. None of Bill's hospitality in Bethlehem to put 'em on and stretch their belts!' Chuckles and 'hear-hear' echoed around the room.

He continued. 'Yo, cool dudes. You gotta remember – when you hit rock bottom you're not alone. The coolest man in history is by your side. You get me? His name is Jesus, and He sings this song to you.' He pressed play again.

'Now if you feel that you can't go on, because all of your hope is gone, and your life is filled with much confusion, until happiness is just an illusion. And your world around is crumblin' down, Darling, reach out, come on girl, reach on out for me, reach out, reach out for me. I'll be there, with a love that will shelter you. I'll be there, with a love that will see you through.' Four Tops: Reach Out 1967

The words of the song touched Carter. His heart pinched with pain. He needed to let go of the past, and to seek out a relationship with this God that these people loved so much.

Halfway through the song, Anna became flustered. Ivanna and Mykyta had their eyes fixed on her as she frantically pressed the buttons on her iPad. 'Yes!' she yelled, and everyone turned to look at her. 'He's here!' She waved the iPad in the air.

'Sorry, sorry,' she laughed as she heard her husband calling to her. She switched the iPad around so that Pavlo could see his children.

'Tato! Tato!' Ivanna made as if to rush to speak to her father, but Mykyta pulled her back and whispered to her in Ukrainian. She stayed still but waved like mad towards the iPad, happy tears trickling down her little chubby cheeks.

The room went back to singing with great gusto. 'I'll be there, with a love that will shelter you. I'll be there, with a love that will see you through.'

When the song finished, Ted waved Matthew in. He walked a little way into the room and stopped. He was holding a walking stick (in place of a shepherd's crook) and put his hand over his eyes and pretended to search for his sheep.

Sharon read some more scripture…

'And there were shepherds living out in the fields nearby, keeping watch over their flocks at night. An angel of the Lord appeared to them, and the glory of the Lord shone around them, and they were terrified.' Luke 2: 8-9 NIV

Emily emerged from the hallway. Her arms spread wide holding out a sheet, meant to be her wings but looking much more like a ghost. On her head a metal coat hanger had been bent into a circle and covered in silver tinsel. Her glittery halo bounced as she flounced down to the shepherd. Matthew flung his arm over his head and cowered, with the overacting skill of a professional.

Sharon tried to muffle a laugh as she continued…

'But the angel said to them, do not be afraid. I bring you good news that will cause great joy for all the people. Today in the town of David a Saviour has been born to you; he is the Messiah, the Lord. This will be a sign to you: You will find a baby wrapped in cloths and lying in a manger.' Luke 2: 10-12 NIV

Matthew and Emily started down the pathway made between the tables.

A tea-towel was tied around his head with string. An old sheet had been cut to drape over his clothes and Bill's dressing gown cord was being used to tie around Matthew's waist. Under one arm he carried his prized possession, a fluffy toy lamb that his father had given him two years ago.

Joanne waved at him as he made his way to the front. He half-smiled back at her. He loved her very much, but God hadn't answered his prayer, his dad wasn't there.

Emily, with all her frailty and yet enthusiastic acting skills, knocked the wood while getting into position in the tiny space.

179

The cardboard star on the top of the stable began to slip. Brian rushed forward and pushed it up again, hastily using more tape to keep it in place. He tiptoed out of the way when he'd finished.

When they settled, Sharon nodded towards the men in the doorway and spoke again...

'After they had heard the king, they went on their way, and the star they had seen when it rose went ahead of them until it stopped over the place where the child was. When they saw the star, they were overjoyed.' Matthew 2: 9-10 NIV

She gave a nod at two children sitting on the front row. They turned on two torches and shone them at the glittery star.

She continued...

'On coming to the house, they saw the child with his mother Mary, and they bowed down and worshipped him. Then they opened their treasures and presented him with gifts of gold, frankincense and myrrh.' Matthew 2: 11 NIV

Ted grinned as he pressed play one last time.

'I thought God was only real in fairy tales, meant for someone else but not for me. Religion wasn't for me, thought it would make me weak. I ignored when he reached out for me. But then I felt His Grace, now I'm a believer! Not a trace, of doubt in my mind. I am loved, I am a believer in my redeemer Jesus Christ.' The Monkeys: I'm a Believer 1966

After the first chorus, the whole pub joined in and sang along. The rafters of the Berry Inn rocked. The atmosphere sizzled like electricity! Who needs power!

Joseph, Carter and Mark positioned themselves around Mary and Joseph. Glitter covered crowns on their heads, sheets over their bodies and pretend gifts in their hands.

While Carter tried to squash his embarrassment, he noticed people's shoulders were shaking. Were they laughing? Yes, they were definitely fighting back laughter, some better than others. Bill and Elmer (who were standing next to each other) both had their hands over their mouths trying to hold it in. But their whole bodies were shaking with laughter.

'What is it?' Carter hissed quietly in Mark's ear.

'Joseph!' was all that Mark could answer as he tried his hardest to hold his laughter in.

Carter glanced to the side at Joseph. He was swaying to the music. Joseph leaned on his stick, but he bounced his shoulders and nodded his head along to the tune, while tapping his good foot. His crown kept slipping and falling over his eyes. He simply shoved it back upright and continued bopping.

I guess three grown men in a nativity is pretty funny, thought Carter. The more he watched Joseph, the more his shoulders began to shake up and down as joy surged through him.

When the song died down, Ted tried to get his laughing under control. When he'd managed it enough to talk, he called out. 'The joy of the Lord be with you.'

'And with you,' half the room called back.

'God gave us the best possible gift, when He gave us His son. But He didn't stop there. Every moment of every day, the

Lord continues to bless people. Now, I have a very special surprise for a very dear little boy…'

The room went quiet and fixed on Ted intently.

'A little bird told me that a certain young man asked God for a miracle. Is that right, *Matthew*?'

Matthew's mouth dropped open as he nodded.

There came a rustle near the door and everyone turned to look.

Liam came in, his hair still wet, and dressed in a tracksuit borrowed from Carter.

'Dad!' Matthew flew down the room and jumped into Liam's arms.

Joanne gasped, her hands flying to her mouth.

'Aww,' escaped the mouths of nearly everyone.

'Dad! Dad, you're here, you're really here!'

Liam put Matthew down and smiled. 'I am son.' Liam looked up and searched the room for Joanne. 'I'm sorry, Jo,' he said with a croak.

She made her way across the room. Later would be the time for questions and answers. Right now all her mind would allow her to say repeatedly was, *Oh, thank you Lord, thank you.*

The three of them embraced in a family hug and the room roared and clapped.

After a few moments, Bill called out. 'Right you lot! The carol singers will be starting shortly, and then after that supper will be served!'

Another cheer went around the room.

JOANNE AND MATTHEW clung to Liam and wouldn't let him go. He explained what had happened, and she rushed him over to a seat near the fire.

'I lost your presents. I'm so sorry. Maybe later Bill will help me find them.'

'No way, you're not going out there again!' Joanne raised a hand and brushed his cheek. 'We only need you.'

'Dad?'

'Yes son?'

'I'm glad you're here. I've missed you.'

Liam patted his knee and Matthew climbed on. 'I've missed you too, very much.'

'Did you get me good presents?'

Joanne and Liam laughed.

'I might have done. Hopefully, we will go and find them at some stage. The wrapping and boxes will have perished, but the toys should be alright.'

'I'm going to say a prayer tonight and ask God to look after them. He answers *my* prayers!'

Liam ruffled his son's hair. 'Mine too.'

Liam and Joanne locked eyes. With them he told her exactly how much he loved her.

AFTER LETTING HER husband speak to the children, Anna shoo'd them away wanting to know how Pavlo was really doing. She settled into the window seat in the quiet room. Pulling her knees up, she leant the iPad against them.

'Tell me.'

'All is good, and will be fine. Our men are very brave. You should see them, Anna. I am proud beyond words. We have agreed between us, our captain and the men, that even if Zelenskyy and Putin should sign a peace agreement, we will *not* stop fighting. We fight for our nation and for our future, for our children's future.'

'How long do you think it will go on?'

'As long as it takes to be free!'

'I am proud of you, Pavlo! I pray the fighting will stop, and we can return to our village. I miss you.'

They talked some more, mostly about how the children were coping.

'I need to go now. I love you, my heart.'

'I love you too, Pavlo.'

Together they said, 'Glory to Ukraine! Glory to the heroes!'

The Holly & the Ivy

Christmas Eve, 2022

THE TWELVE SINGERS wrapped themselves up and put on Hyacinth's red hats. Four of them carried crusade lanterns with latticed-glass. The candles within flickered brightly. They gathered together in front of the main entrance and started singing, quietly at first and then building in volume and confidence.

'Hark! The herald angels sing, Glory to the new-born king

Peace on earth and mercy mild, God and sinners reconciled

Joyful all ye nations rise, Join the triumph of the skies

With angelic host proclaim, Christ is born in Bethlehem

Hark! The herald angels sing, Glory to the new-born king.'

By the second line the front door opened and the villagers crowded around the doorway to listen to them. At the end of the second verse, they began to make their way through to the main lounge. The only other sound heard was a bang as the door closed.

The villagers sat and stood, listening to the choir with rosy faces and warm hands and hearts. They could have been alone at home, in the cold. Instead, they were gathered together as one family.

As they started the third verse everyone began to join in.

The carollers walked across the room and stood to the left of the piano. Warm, they quickly took off their coats, but as secretly agreed earlier they all kept their red woolly hats on.

Carter looked to Laura and she gave him the go-ahead nod. His fingers flew across the keys as The Holly and the Ivy was played. Everyone who knew the words joined in, and in all honesty the choir was there only to guide them and try to keep them in tune – something which was practically impossible.

Next came God Rest you Merry Gentlemen, followed by Deck the Halls with Boughs of Holly.

Laura took a step forward. 'Hi everyone, I just want to say thank you very much for being with us today. Whatever transpired to bring you here I want you to know we're very glad to have you.' Laura gave a shy smile to Carter. 'Thank you also for all the donations you've been making. I can't believe how much money you've all put in the bucket on the counter.'

'Joseph's put in an I.O.U written on a paper napkin,' called out Martha.

Maeve gave Martha a scowl. 'I'm sure he's good for it.'

'I'll hold him to it,' called Mark. 'No fishing it out now, Joseph, we've all seen it.'

Laughs went around the room.

'As if!' grumbled Joseph.

'Anyway, thank you, everyone. You are all appreciated.'

'Sing us another carol, love,' called out Mark, sending his wife Sue a wink.

'Really?' said Laura pretending that she didn't want to.

Everyone roared. 'One more, just one more!'

'OK. OK,' she laughed. 'Just one more, and then I'm off to help Dad with your supper!' She grinned at Ted, who gave her a thumb's up. He'd warned her that people always wanted more and the last song delay had been planned.

'O Holy night! The stars are brightly shining, It is the night of our dear Saviour's birth. Long lay the world in sin and error pining, 'til He appears and the soul felt its worth.

A thrill of hope the weary world rejoices, For yonder breaks a new and glorious morn. Fall on your knees; O hear the Angel voices! O night divine, O night when Christ was born. O night, O Holy night, O night divine!'

This time the crowd didn't join in. They didn't want to spoil the beautiful song and left the carollers to bless their ears.

They received a standing ovation when they finished. Spontaneously, the choir all took off their hats and threw them in the air.

'Right, now let's get some scran!' called Sharon.

TWO HOURS LATER, Carter and Laura stood side-by-side next to the huge industrial sinks in the kitchen washing dishes together.

'I bet you never expected to be washing dishes in a pub on Christmas Eve, did you?'

For a moment he didn't answer, and then he lifted his head and drew her gaze to his face. 'This whole time here has been amazing. I won't lie; it's the complete opposite to what I was hoping for! But I'm glad. I think Cumbria has become my second home.'

He searched her eyes. *Do you want me? Should I stay?*

'I'm very glad you came,' she whispered.

He bent his head, his eyes intent on her lips. She closed her eyes and rose on her tiptoes slightly to meet him.

'This is the last of them,' announced Sharon, coming into the kitchen with a tray of dirty glasses.

Carter and Laura chuckled as they pulled apart.

'GO ON LAURA, GET your dad to sing for us!' cried out Martha.

From behind the bar Bill waved a frantic 'no' with his arms.

Martha persisted. 'Please, Bill. It's been so long. Give us a tune.'

Father and daughter locked eyes.

Laura simply knew it was time. She gave a nod.

'Yikes, I've not sung solo for years. You all might regret this in a moment!'

A clap went up in the room.

Bill came out from behind the bar and went to sit at the piano. He thought his fingers might freeze up, but they remembered even though he'd thought he'd forgotten.

Laura came to stand beside him and put her hand on his shoulder for encouragement.

'What shall I sing, love?'

'Mum's favourite, The Christmas Song.'

He turned his head to look at her. 'Sure?'

'Sure.'

He played a few bars and then started singing. 'Chestnuts roasting on an open fire...'

Both Laura and Bill had tears running down their cheeks by the time Bill got to 'although it's been said, many times many ways, merry Christmas to you.' But they were happy tears of remembrance.

The room went mad clapping like billy-o when he finished.

'More, more,' they called out.

'Yeah, but for rhubarb's sake... make it something cheerful,' grumbled Joseph.

It's a Wonderful Life

Christmas Day, 2022

At six a.m. laura's alarm started buzzing, although she'd been awake for a while. A to-do list by the side of the bed reminded her of all the things requiring her attention today. After having a speedy shower, she dressed in comfortable jeans, a t-shirt with 'Ho! Ho! Ho!' splashed on the front, and a warm Aran cardigan. She pinned her hair up and peered at her face in the mirror. If she had time later before they sat down to eat, she would run upstairs and put a little makeup on. It was Christmas Day after all! But for now there was too much to get done. She picked up a box full of festive headbands off the dresser, and then opened her door as quietly as she could.

Last night, most of the people had gone home, but a few had stayed. Liam, Joanne and Matthew had been given a room. Bill wouldn't take 'no' for an answer. He'd been worried about Liam and hadn't wanted him to go out in the cold. Elmer had also been persuaded to stay overnight, and Joseph surprised everyone when he'd declared he could have the spare bed in his room. He'd grumbled something under his breath about it taking any mad ideas out of Maeve's head.

Nearly everyone else had confirmed if the electricity was still off, they would return in the morning. With no power, today would be harder than yesterday when they'd had the generator. Still, it was all workable. Two huge turkeys had been set to cook overnight in the Aga, so if nothing else they could all have turkey sandwiches for lunch.

Closing the door with great care to try and stop it squeaking, she double-checked the corridor was clear and tiptoed along the carpet. Gosh, but it was cold!

As her foot hit the first step of the stairs she heard a creak and turned around. Smiling at her, and also on his toes was Carter.

'Merry Christmas,' he mouthed.

She grinned and mouthed it back.

Like ninja warriors they made their way to the kitchen.

'Wow, it's warm in here, and it smells divine,' said Carter as they went in.

'That's the turkeys. I'll take them out, and then pop the kettle on. That's one of the best things about the Aga, it's always warm and mornings smell heavenly.

Laura put her box on a shelf and then pulled on huge oven gloves and removed the turkeys. 'I'll leave the foil on for now.' She filled the kettle with water. 'Anyway, you're up early.'

'I couldn't sleep.'

'Me neither.' After switching the kettle on to boil, she turned around to look at him properly.

How he'd changed in the time he'd been with them!

'I wanted to buy you a present, only I wasn't expecting to get snowed in.'

'Oh, I'm glad you didn't. We haven't given presents in a long time. You know what they say – your presence is more valuable than your presents. We mean it. Too many families get into credit card debt due to buying things they can't afford. I don't mean the children of course. If I had children I would want to buy them something; maybe not hundreds of pounds worth, but something special.'

'I take it that means you would like children one day?'

'Very much, I'd really love a big family. How about you?'

'Until recently I didn't even want to get married.'

Suddenly, colour flooded both their cheeks.

'Ah, I see I'm not the first up. Merry Christmas you two!'

'Merry Christmas, Dad.'

'Merry Christmas, Bill!'

'You're just in time for a cuppa.'

With tea and coffee made, they sat around the table and took a moment.

Bill took a sip of tea and then asked, 'Have you tried the landline?'

'It was the first thing I did. It's still down unfortunately.'

'How many do you think will return today?' asked Carter.

'Most of them that were here yesterday will come back. Not the Sheldons, Ramsey or Tucker. They all have Agas and coal fires and they mentioned yesterday they wanted to stay at home. I think everyone else is coming back.'

'So, quite a few for dinner again then,' said Carter.

'For sure. I can't make a traditional roast like I planned; there will be too many of us. But I have a good buffet planned out with a mix of hot and cold food, thanks to the Aga.'

'We'll need to stock up a lot on coal and wood,' said Laura. 'Would you like to help me with that?'

Carter grinned, 'Sure.'

Bill looked between them and shook his head. *Ah, young love*, he thought to himself.

Just then Sharon came in. 'Merry Christmas everyone!'

They all returned the greeting.

She grabbed a cup of tea and pulled out a chair next to Bill.

'You're early,' said Bill.

'I think the cold woke me up. My nose was like ice when I touched it. The rest of me was toasty though, under the covers.'

They chatted and planned, while enjoying their first drink of the day.

'I'm going to light the fires in the main room and breakfast lounge,' said Sharon. 'I don't think it will be long before others turn up. I'll light a couple of lamps as well.'

Laura stood up. 'We'll start by bringing in the coal and wood, when we've stocked up as much as we can, I'll come back and help in the kitchen.'

Carter got up. 'See you soon,' he grinned at Bill and Sharon.

At the bottom of the stairs, Laura looked at him with twinkling eyes. 'You ready to get cold again? The stash is in the shed, it's going to take several trips.'

'I best get my arctic outfit then, by the door in ten?'

'See you then.'

Automatically their hands reached for each other, they didn't hold hands. They simply let the backs of their hands brush together. For now it was enough.

THE HORDES BEGAN ARRIVING just before seven. Most of them apologised for being so early, but it was just too cold at home.

They piled into the kitchen until no more would fit in.

Bill waved a tea-towel around. 'Off into the lounge with you lot. I'll have a breakfast buffet going in the small lounge in about an hour.'

Several people offered to stay and help, which Bill gratefully accepted.

Father Christmas (aka Joanne and Alfred after a dash home on the tractor) had visited the pub during the night and left Matthew some presents by the tree.

Anna had explained that she and the children would celebrate again on the seventh of January. Bill and Laura had wrapped a few presents for them and put them under the tree, and Anna was happy for the kids to open them today.

With the fires going in both rooms, and the Aga on maximum in the kitchen, the downstairs of the building stayed cosy and warm.

Breakfast was jolly and full of chatter. The box of festive headbands and crowns got passed around and most people wore one. Laura put one on that was a bunch of holly and baubles. Carter accepted antler ears, but the little brass bells kept jingling every time he moved so he kept taking it off. It was a step too festive for him!

After they'd eaten, everyone pitched in and helped clean and wash up and then moved straight on to prepare for lunch, which would be the main meal of the day.

A team of ladies worked side-by-side making some turkey and cheese sandwiches, which they wrapped and put in the cool outhouse for the evening tea. They all wore headbands that consisted of elf ears and pointed green hats. With no electricity they decided to make their own music and began a list of songs that started with Rocking around the Christmas Tree and led into Jingle Bells.

Maeve and Martha organised party games in the lounge and they started the day off with charades.

When lunch was called, everyone was ready for it. The foodie smells filling the pub all day had been delicious.

'Before we pile into the small lounge for some food,' called Bill above the excited chatter. 'I would like to say a prayer.'

Slowly, the room hushed and everyone sat down again, leaving only Bill standing.

'Most of you know that since my Olivia died, nearly five years ago, I have struggled a lot. I even lost my faith at one point.' He stopped to gulp and draw a deep breath.

'I thought because I'd not been able to help Olivia, and because the bottle had called my name and I'd answered, that I was useless. But I've come to know that as a lie.' He paused for a moment and looked around the room.

'No one is useless in this world that lightens the burden of another. It is in helping one another that love is expressed and joy found.' Bill laid his hand on the top of the Bible he held in his other hand. 'Within these pages lies the greatest story ever told. That God loved us so much, He gave his one and only son unto the cross so that we might live. Across the world, nativities have been performed by children...'

'And adults!' yelled out Ted.

'Yes, and in some plays even adults. But who are they but children at heart!'

'Hear, hear,' called out several people.

Martha took Maeve's hand in hers and gave it a gentle squeeze.

Laura slipped her hand into Carter's.

Bill waited for the room to go still once more. 'These last few days, love in action has rippled through the homes of Berrycombe. I very much doubt we will ever be the same.'

'Lord, I hope not!' squeaked Maeve, winking at Joseph.

'I just want to say thank you to the Lord for allowing me to be here to witness how you've all put Christmas together. It has been a privilege to be part of this festive banding together.'

'*Vicar* Bill, will you please bless us so that we can go and eat?' cried Hyacinth.

Everyone laughed.

Bill raised his hand holding the Bible and everyone went quiet. 'Lord, we thank you for your many phenomenal blessings, but for the gift of your Son we thank you the most. Bless everyone here today and grant that we may move closer to you more and more each day. For ever and ever…'

And everyone said… 'Amen.'

LUNCH WAS A HUGE SUCCESS. Warm turkey and hot pigs in blankets, went down with yesterday's pastries and a bowl of hot vegetable soup. Everyone had brought along their food from home, so there were plenty of different puddings to choose from. Including Christmas cake, Yule log and sherry trifles.

Laura refused to let their only paying guest wash up afterwards, and sent him off to find something more pleasant to do. Honestly, standing next to her was the most pleasant thing he could think of to do, but he graciously accepted her pushing him away and went to join the others in the lounge.

He found an empty chair next to Joseph by the fireplace.

'How you doing? Is your ankle OK?'

'It's not so bad. Walking is easier. I've had a reet good time here, I have. But I'm looking forward to me own bed tomorrow night.'

'Do you get lonely, living there on your own?'

Joseph sighed, 'Sure miss my Daisy, I do. But there's no place like home, her memories are all around me there. What about you, young man? Do you think you're going to miss all this when you go home?'

Carter shifted his weight in the chair and tried to get comfortable, though it was the conversation that really put him ill at ease and not the padded seat. 'They say all good things come to an end.'

'That doesn't answer my question. Wouldn't you like to stay?'

'I've been on my own ever since I was seventeen. I'm worried I'm too set in my ways to change now.'

Joseph shot him a sideways glance and then leaned forward in his chair. He picked up the fire tongs and used them to lift a single piece of flaming coal out of the fireplace. He checked to see if Carter was watching him, and then lay the coal down on the hearth on its own.

Carter raised one eyebrow but didn't say anything.

Joseph re-hung the tongs and sat back in the chair. 'We aren't supposed to be on our own.' His eyes remained fixed on the coal lump, that was dying and slowly going out.

'You live on your own.'

Joseph snorted. 'Where am I now?'

'Yes, but you don't live here.'

'Who runs me to hospital? Who picks me up every Thursday and drives me to town so I can go shopping? Who cuts my hedge for me in spring? Who brings me around a roast dinner every Sunday? Do you know?'

Carter shook his head.

'My friends. They are my extended family. I might live in that cottage on my own, but I'm never alone. I only need pick up the phone and I can talk to someone.'

'I guess that's where village life differs from the city,' answered Carter.

'No, I don't think that's it. You can have extended family in the city too. The difference is *you* and the choices you make.'

Kids' laughter in the background mixed with adult chatter, all clamouring to be heard over the never-ending laughing and shouting over various board games.

The old man and the American sat lost in the noise, both staring at a black lump of coal that had lost all its life.

After a while, Joseph asked, 'Will you put the coal back on the fire?'

The coal sat alone and cold.

Carter used the tongs to pick it up, and placed the lifeless lump back on the fire. Within moments flames began to flicker from it once again.

The meaning of it warmed Carter's heart more than the flames warmed his body.

'Thank you,' he said to Joseph getting up.

'Aye, you're welcome so you are. And, Son,' he reached up and touched Carter's arm. When Carter looked at him he grinned. 'I sure hope that you're going to become a part of my extended family. But even if you don't, I would have you remember this one thing: Pain, if responded to correctly, turns into compassion. And sorrow, when mature, is a soul-builder that propels you into the Lord's Grace.'

Carter tensed his lips, as emotions rose. He gave a short nod and went off in search of Laura. He needed to talk to her.

'CAN WE TALK?' Carter asked Laura as she untied her apron.

Her smile dropped a little. 'Is everything alright?'

'Yes, it's just… I'd like…'

'To have a chat?'

Carter's shoulders slumped as he took a deep breath. 'Yes, if that's OK.'

'Of course it is. Let's go to the quiet room, no one will be there.'

When Laura closed the door, Carter felt himself freeze up. He shoved his hands in his pockets and looked out of the window.

She came to his side and gently tugged his arm. He glanced down at her. She showed him her hand. He smiled and pulled his out of his pocket and took hold of her hand.

For a moment they stood in peaceful quiet, gazing at the white wonderland.

Eventually, Carter turned from the window to look at her.

'I know we haven't known each other very long, but I wanted to let you know that I, that I…' He coughed.

Laura brought her other hand around so that she held Carter's hand in both of hers. Warmth flooded him with the loving touch. A surge of excitement rose in his chest.

'I really like you!'

Laura laughed, 'Aye, that's a reet gammy romantic you are.'

'I am?'

'Yes,' she laughed.

'Is that a good or bad thing?'

'Depends. I said you're a right rotten romantic, so if I was looking for a Romeo I don't think you'd do.'

'Oh!' His face fell and he looked at the floor.

'However, as I run a mile from Romeos, and as I'm only interested in real gentlemen, I guess you're doing OK.'

He squinted at her. 'You sure?'

She reached up on tiptoes and was just putting her lips against his… when the door opened.

'Oops sorry,' said Sharon. 'I was just doing a search for dirty dishes.'

Laura moved away from Carter. 'There's none in here,' she smiled.

'Sorry, sorry,' said Sharon backing out of the room and shutting the door quietly.

Just then the sun broke out from behind the clouds. Both of them turned to look.

A crisp, bright rainbow bent across a sky that was half grey and half black. The beauty of its colours lit up sky and hope flooded the room.

'I have so much to tell you, so much to explain. I no longer want to shut the world out. Someone reminded me just now that we only have one life to live. I don't know how long it will take me to drop all my old ways, and I know I need to read the Bible and get to know God. And you might not want someone who is awfully damaged like me, but...'

Laura put a finger over his lips to stop him from talking. 'I really like you too, Carter. I thank God that He delivered you to us. Stop worrying so much. Let's take it a moment at a time and see what unfolds.'

'That sounds wonderful.' He pushed a piece of hair that had fallen out of her bun off her face. 'There's a phone call I have to make. Will you ask everyone to wait for me before they take the envelopes off the tree?'

'Of course.'

A Cup of Kindness

Christmas Day, 2022

CARTER'S FINGERS SHOOK as he pressed the screen on his mobile. He put the phone to his ear and waited. One ring, two rings, three…

'Hello?' The gentle voice sounded curious.

Carter's voice came out like a croak. 'Mom.'

Five seconds of silence felt like an eternity.

Hesitant, 'Carter?'

'Hi mom.' A firework display cracked open his ribs. Years of squashed emotions, of refusing to love or be loved came flooding to the fore. He sat down and fought back the tears that had rushed to his eyes.

'Carter!' The voice now had a high-pitched squeak. 'Carter, is that really you?'

'I'm sorry it's been so long.'

'Carter! Danny! It's Carter!'

'What?' Carter heard a man call. 'Really?' She must have nodded because Carter didn't hear a reply. 'Can I have the phone?' There came a crackle as their landline phone was passed to his adoptive father. 'Carter?'

'Hello Dad.'

'Oh son!'

Carter heard his mom burst into tears. It was too much for him and he could hold his own back no more. They soaked his face as they ran unchecked.

'Dad, I've phoned to say sorry for how I've behaved and for not appreciating you.'

'No need, son, no need.' Daniel's voice came out hoarse and choked. 'You know we love you, will always love you. You don't have to be here to be in our hearts.'

It was too much. Carter lowered the phone. His head dropped to his chest, as he struggled with letting go of pain and guilt.

Julie came back on the phone. Her muffled voice called out to him, 'Carter, are you there?'

He put the phone back to his ear. 'Yes Mom.'

'Why have you called? Are you alright? Are you ill? Shall I fly to New York? I'll come as soon as I can.'

'I'm fine, and actually I'm not at home, I'm in England.'

'Really? Well that is just marvellous!'

Carter knew her excitement came from the fact he'd left his apartment. 'I wanted to let you know that I think I've met the woman I'm going to marry. I haven't asked her yet, and honestly we haven't known each other long, but I know she's the one for me. The funny thing is… I deliberately chose the

Berry Inn because they advertised they didn't celebrate Christmas. Yet, the last few days have been crammed with a host of festive activities.' He knew he had brushed over the first part of the statement really quickly. It had sounded strange to say aloud what had been in his mind for the last week.

She was openly sobbing. 'I'm so happy, Carter, so happy.'

'Mom, I'm sorry I left home the way I did.'

'You have your own life to live, we know that. We just want you to be happy.'

'I think for the first time in my life happiness seems like a possibility.' Then guilt, that it sounded like he hadn't been happy with them, hit him. He rushed on, 'I don't mean anything by that, I...'

'Carter, it's fine. We understand. We honestly do. But I have to tell you something.'

'OK.'

'Last Christmas Eve your Dad had an epiphany and went straight to his knees to pray a specific prayer. He asked God that by Christmas this year, you would know Him. Has that happened? Has Christ come into your life?'

He knew the answer immediately, but it was hard to get the word out due to the amount of emotion. 'Yes.'

She squealed, yelled, and then sobbed.

Daniel came back on the phone. 'Carter, whenever you're ready we would love to see you again.'

'I'll be with you early in the New Year.'

'Well, that sure would be terrific. You've made us both very happy.'

'I need to go, but I'll phone again soon.'

'Merry Christmas, Son.'

'Merry Christmas, Carter!' Julie yelled.

'Merry Christmas.' As soon as he'd hung up, joy flooded through him, a confirmation that he had done the right thing at last. There was a lot of work ahead of him with reconnect to them, but he knew now without a shadow of a doubt that he did love them. Perhaps had always loved them, but hadn't known how to express it.

AFTER HE'D SPLASHED water on his face, Carter went bounding downstairs.

'He's here!' called Sharon.

'What's going on?' asked Carter.

Laura handed him his festive headband. 'We're just going to run outside and take a quick photo. Dad's set up his tripod and the camera will be turned on using the remote, so we can all be in it. It's Sharon's idea. It's so we can put a new picture on the wall.'

'Aren't we putting our coats on?'

'No, Dad's all set up. We'll rush outside say cheers, and rush back in again.'

'But it's just started to snow again!'

'Don't be a wuss!' laughed Laura. 'We'll only be a moment, and Dad wants to capture all our different Christmas jumpers and headbands.'

'Do *I have* to wear one?'

'But antlers look so cute on you!'

He pulled a face, but being a good sport he put them on. 'Whatever you do, Lizzie can *never,* ever, see this picture!' As he moved his head the bells on it jingled.

Within moments everyone had flooded through the doors and gathered on the steps leading up to the pub. Bill had set the tripod up down the path so the photo would include the sign over the door that read, The Berry Inn.

'Ready everyone, say Christmas!'

'Christmas!' they all cried out and Bill pressed the camera's remote control.

Immediately, everyone started rushing back inside.

'Let me fetch the camera for you,' said Carter and went charging down the cleared pathway.

On the way, Carter's foot slipped. His arms pin-wheeled like crazy and he crashed to the ground with a thud. 'Crushed raspberries! That hurt!'

Laura and Bill, who'd rushed over to help him up, stopped and stared at him. Then the two of them, instead of helping him up, gave him a slow clap.

Carter got to his knees and pushed himself up. 'Why the clap?'

'Because you're finally a member of Berrycombe's fruit and vegetable club,' laughed Bill.

'I am?' Carter scratched his head. 'How did that happen?'

Laura came up to him and hooked her arm through his, giving him a tug so they would head back to the inn. 'You see, it's not *what* you say that's important, but *how* you say it.'

'Oh!'

Bill picked up the camera tripod, and then hooked one arm through Carter's other arm. As they walked towards the building, Carter's shoulders started to shake. By the time they'd reached the door, all three of them were roaring their heads off.

BACK INSIDE, BILL fetched a large pan of mulled wine that had been simmering on top of the Aga. As he took it into the lounge, the smell of cinnamon, cloves, and oranges filled the room.

Glasses were filled and passed around.

Carter accepted his and wrapped his hands around the warm glass. 'If you could bottle this smell and sell it, you'd make a fortune!'

'Wait till you taste it. It's alcohol-free wine so the children can have some, but the flavour is just yummy.'

'This is the best birthday I've ever had,' said Carter.

'What! It's your birthday? Why didn't you say?'

'I never celebrate it. I'm not sure why I mentioned it, only today has been amazing.'

'Hey everyone…'

'Oh no don't!' Carter flapped his hand at her.

'Everyone, it's Carter's birthday today!'

'Whoop-whoop, and happy birthday,' filled the room.

'You kept that quiet, son.'

'I don't celebrate it.'

'Too late for that now,' said Bill. 'Happy birthday to you, happy birthday to you…' The whole pub joined in with much gusto. Their enthusiasm and acceptance drowned the memories of the past… maybe Joseph's wisdom was right, no man is an island don't they say?

'Time to grab yourself an envelope off the tree,' called out Sharon.

People hurried to the tree.

Matthew wanted the one right at the top of the tree. Liam lifted him up so he could reach it.

Carter and Laura hung back until everyone else had taken one.

While they waited, Carter took a moment to look out of the window at the fluttering of snowflakes. The memory of the flake against his window-pane last year came to him. That had been the moment something inside him had snapped. From then he had started questioning his reason for living. The absence of love in his life had swelled and consumed him. Deep inside he'd known he wasn't living the life he was supposed to. He'd cut himself off from the world and the light of love, not wanting to be hurt ever again.

How is it, he contemplated, *that a man can be alive but dead inside?* Resolution rose in his chest. *No more and hopefully never again.* He sneaked a quick glance at Laura who was standing beside him. She filled his chest with warmth and happiness; he just hoped he would be able to do the same for her.

Maeve came to stand beside him. 'I've been thinking,' she said.

'What about?'

'I think you're just perfect for our Laura.'

Carter pulled a face. 'I haven't exactly had a perfect life.'

Mauve snorted. 'Oh sweetheart, there is no such thing as a perfect life. All we ever have are little tiny flawless *moments*. And if a person is wise, they take all those memories and create a beautiful web with them. Then they can look back at the end of their life and be satisfied. True wisdom, dear boy,' she leaned over and patted his arm, 'is seeing what's in front of you before it has gone.'

Carter looked at Laura who had turned slightly and was chatting away with Martha. He turned back to Maeve. 'I hope that I'll be able to make her happy, I will certainly try my very best.'

Maeve smiled. 'No one can do any more than that.'

Laura stopped talking to Martha and turned to him.

'Shall we?'

He gave a nod and the two of them approached the tree. There were six envelopes left for them to choose from.

NORMALLY A MASTER OF WORDS, the short sentence on his card dumbfounded him. His chest exploded with a lightning strike; the card trembled in his hand.

God loves <u>you</u> so much, that He let his only Son die on the cross.

He understood, and in that moment truly accepted.

He turned his wrist and checked the time.

'You need to be somewhere?' laughed Bill waving to him from the bar.

Joy had filled Carter's chest. 'Indeed not. I merely wanted to note the time that my life changed forever.'

'Er?' grunted Bill shaking his head.

As with explorers of great new worlds, Carter marvelled at his discovery, the fact that people do still believe in the reason for the season. All he'd ever had to do was to peek behind the wrapping paper, tinsel and fairy lights, and he would have seen love in action. He'd just never looked.

A forty-year-old Carter stood with his back against the wall and watched the people who had brought him back to life. Gratitude for each and every one of them swelled in his chest, because for the first time in his life *he* believed in the reason for Christmas. Tears stung his eyes, he blinked them away.

Laura touched his arm. 'Everything OK?'

Since arriving in England, his face once angular and stiff had morphed into a glow of radiant softness. The copious amount of hearty, healthy food he'd had eaten since arriving had also put a little fat back on his body. He looked a million times better for it. An outward display mirroring the change in his spirit.

Overcome with love and thankfulness, he cupped Laura's face in his hands. 'Everything is awesome.' Letting go of her, he reached over to the mantel. He tugged a small piece of mistletoe off the wreath and slipped it in the wreath-headband on her head. Then he did something he'd been longing to do since the first time he saw her. He wrapped his arms around her and pulled her gently to him – and kissed her. She wrapped her arms around his neck and lost herself in their first kiss.

A single tear rolled down Bill's cheek as he watched Carter hold and kiss his daughter. 'Ho, ho, ho, Merry Christmas!' he yelled, one arm wrapped around Sharon's shoulders, and his other brandishing a glass of Baileys.

The room erupted with cheerful accord.

'Merry Christmas everyone!'

Thank you so much for reading A White Christmas in Berrycombe. I hope you enjoyed Carter & Laura's Christmas story.

If you have time to pop a review onto Amazon I would really appreciate it, reader's words of encouragement mean the world to me.

Sincerely, Tracy Traynor

A blessing: from my house to yours at Christmas time and always.

In loneliness – may you find a friend

In poverty – may generosity abound

In sickness – may strength be granted

In uncertainty – may wisdom light your path

In absence – may love take root

In grief – may your joy surge and swell

In doubt – may assurance rise up

In fear – may angels guard your back

In cold – may love warm your heart and

In life – may faith show you the way

Author Information

If you'd like to know more about my books, please check out my web.

http://www.tntraynor.uk

If you would like to receive updates by receiving my email newsletter, please sign up at https://sendfox.com/tntraynor

In my newsletter will be updates about my books, book competitions, a book review from me and eBooks that are on offer or free by other authors. The newsletter is only quarterly, so only 4 a year ☺ no spam or sharing of details.

If you enjoyed this book you might also enjoy some of my other books:

Christian Historical Fiction – Women of Courage Series

https://www.amazon.com/Women-Courage-4-Book/dp/B091TTXQ6V

MULTI AWARD WINNING SERIES

Standalone Stories with a theme of courage and love

WOMEN OF COURAGE

| 1912 - 1985 Inspired by the life of Moira Smith | 1904 - 1905 Inspired by the Welsh Revival | 2020 A Love Story | 1958 A story of hope | 1666 A story of faith |

Printed in Great Britain
by Amazon

37523003R00126